Under the Eaves
Reflections of an Ordinary Life

Under the Eaves

Reflections of

an Ordinary Life

Evelyn B. Michaud

Copyright © 2005 by Evelyn B. Michaud.

ISBN :   Hardcover   1-4134-6230-8
         Softcover   1-4134-6229-4

All rights reserved. No part of this book may be reproduced or transmitted in any form or by any means, electronic or mechanical, including photocopying, recording, or by any information storage and retrieval system, without permission in writing from the copyright owner.

This book was printed in the United States of America.

To order additional copies of this book, contact:
Xlibris Corporation
1-888-795-4274
www.Xlibris.com
Orders@Xlibris.com

25698

CONTENTS

Acknowledgments 11
The Little Voice 14
Grey Clapboards 17
Under The Eaves 24
Duggan School 29
Sulfur Powder 36
Baloney Curls 40
The South Leonard Street Bus 44
Winter Wash Day 48
Drying Mittens 52
The Lake Cottage 56
The Four Holer 61
The Virgin Mary 64
Discovering More Than Sand and Sun 70
Pink Satin 75
The Rose Of Sharon 78
I Was a Privileged Child 83
The Camping Trip 88
Uncle Vic 94
The Pink Suit 98
The White House 102
The Dance 106
To my first Grandchild 110
October Sunshine 114
October Mist 118
Barren Branches 123
Coming and Going 126
Flower Pots 130
There's Always "Hope" 134

The Builder	143
Life is Like a Profit and Loss Statement	147
Neighbors	151
Waiting Rooms	155
She Only Came Once	160
Old Kids	164
The Song Bird	168
Business Cards	171
The First One	175
The Christmas Tree	179
A Wee One	183
Showing Off	186
Post Script or Four is Never Enough	189

To my children and grandchildren whose lives and love delight me and sustain me each and every day and especially to the little voice who said, "Grammy, you should be a writer."

Thanks also to my husband who continues to provide the encouragement to go on with my dream and to my assorted friends and relatives both living and dead who provide so much of the material for my stories.

I am so very grateful.

"The woods are lovely dark and deep
but I have promises to keep
and miles to go before I sleep,
and miles to go before I sleep."

                                                    Robert Frost

Acknowledgments

This book, *Under The Eaves, Reflections of an Ordinary Life* has been in the making for as long as I can remember. It is a dream that I have carried inside of me since childhood. Looking back I remember vividly living in my "attic" room and sitting on the linoleum floor, pen in hand looking out at the railroad tracks across the street and dreaming and imagining what it would be like to be a real writer.

This journey and the process of my book has been helped along the way by countless individuals. Some fleeting acquaintances like my partner in "The Dance." Other individuals whose lives have shaped me and made me realize that in fact, I could be a writer.

I was shaped by parents who were creative in their story telling. From my earliest recollections mom and dad would tell me over and over again about our family, the house I lived in, the cottage we occupied at Hitchcock Lake, the ceremonies of life and death, the times of joy and sorrow. Mom continues to this day to remind me about those times and even now at age ninety five relates one or two new stories even some with new characters.

And so I begin to thank all of those people, mom and dad for their stories and the chance to find my creative beginnings. Also at the top of my list is my husband John who has provided encouragement translated into hours of typing the stories, "fixing" things that went wrong with the PC, listening to each and every story while I tried to get it just right.

My children have repeatedly encouraged my writing and have been the recipients of many of my poems and letters as have been our friends and neighbors. All of these people not so gently pushed me to complete this manuscript.

My children John, Heather, Steven and Christopher kept telling me that I just had to write this book. With each hug I would hear phrases like, "Aw, come on mom you can do it." I would also like to thank my Massachusetts daughter Melanie for her excitement at knowing the book was ready to be sent to the publishers.

In addition, thank you to my teachers in Duggan Grammar School those many years ago who gave me gold stars for stories I had written and allowed me to read them to the class.

Finally, to my grandchildren, Elisabeth, Sarah, Alexander and our Massachusetts grandchildren Meghan and Brian for just being in my life. They can illicit creativity from their grandmother in no time at all.

And finally I would like to thank my proof reader, Janice McSwyny for her help in making the final product readable.

The Little Voice

The Little Voice

Over and over again Elisabeth repeats the words, "Grandma, you should be a writer." She is still a little girl who is only now beginning to read on her own, beginning to feel the importance of the printed word. Only now understanding the significance of books in our lives, the magic to be found between the pages.

The little voice repeats again, "You could write stories and I could be the illustrator." Once more I ponder her words. How does this child know my heart, how can she tell it's what I want to do? For all of her young life, all six years of it she has been rocked to sleep listening to Grammy's stories.

"Tell me more please before I go to sleep. Tell me stories of long ago when you were little, tell me stories when my momma was little." And so I begin. I relate stories with characters and plots, some amusing which make her giggle, some just interesting going over the fine details in order to paint a picture for her. She snuggles closer to me and oftentimes puts her head on my shoulder.

I am pleased that she is so interested in storytelling since I grew up in a house full of storytelling and books. I learned from my parents and as I grew older the stories became more important to me too. Life, I was told is like a chapter book with no end.

For many years it has been my dream to become a writer. I wanted to share stories with others, to allow myself the opportunity to put words together and to entwine feelings, memories, thoughts that I wanted to be written. Thoughts and feelings that one day someone else would read and think, "This is just like I feel."

All families have stories, all families talk and share moments from each others lives that's why *Roots* was one of my all time favorite TV programs. I am fascinated by other families and the dynamics that show themselves from the interaction of it's members.

Even as a child I listened intently to the older members of our family relating stories of their lives. In fact, I think I was really more comfortable with older people than with my contemporaries. They just seemed to be a whole lot more interesting.

Our children too were raised with older people. At an early age they were introduced to the special bond between a child and a grandparent or great grandparent, great aunt or uncle. There they found a tie to another era, a dialog with someone so different than themselves. I am glad that they did.

I take my direction not only from within, but from my children and grandchildren. I take pen in hand and begin the journey through my life, my experiences. I type the words I hope will be read. I listen for a little voice that says, "Grammy tell me another story of long ago when you were small."

Grey Clapboards

Grey Clapboards

I was raised in a gray clapboard house that sat on the busy city street known as South Leonard Street, across from the railroad yards, in between Fifth and Sixth Streets, down the street from Rizzuti's Grocery Store, on the bus line and nestled in between other homes of similar character. All these years later and many homes in between, I can still close my eyes and recall exactly how it looked both inside and out and if called upon to recreate it could do so with little difficulty. It is to my credit that I have the uncanny ability even now to step into someone's home and years later to recall in finite detail all of the belongings and their placement within the home.

Having lived in the gray clapboard house (Number 222) for all of my formative years and because so many of my memories would take shape there, that to remember in vibrant detail is not necessarily so uncommon. Of course people say that as one ages the memories of long ago come more to the front and those of just last week vanish quickly. Also, I had the chance to live in a home that itself contained a vast store of memories already built up and communicated to me by my mother who had lived here herself in her formative years. Therefore this house that would provide both shelter and love had almost taken on a character and personality of its own.

The gray clapboard house had seen birth and death, tears of great joy and sorrow, family celebrations, a coming an age for males and females, and a transformation both in physical and spiritual character. When we finally left and gave up the home to the bulldozer, it remained in my mind a gray clapboard house.

My mother had moved there when she was very young and had lived the greatest part of her life within those walls. It was here that the stories she would later tell me were created. Even now I remember those stories of long ago. The house held numerous characters some related and some not. There were the relatives who lived upstairs and the tenants turned "almost family" that lived down. The Italian family would have six children crowded into the five rooms and left to have their seventh in a more upscale neighborhood. Mom was the babysitter for these children and then they were the babysitter for my brother and I and then I for their children and then these children for my children. And on it went. When they left "Uncle Bill and Aunt Bessie" arrived, there to remain until "Uncle Bill" retired from the railroad and they returned to Pennsylvania. After that it would be a succession of other families who would be welcomed into our family until the last tenant left and we remained behind to pack up our belongings and our memories and move on leaving the gray clapboard home to the wrecking crew.

The house was your typical Victorian two family, more narrow than wide, with several porches added to the front and back of the house. It stood squarely between a three family on one side and another three family on the other, separated only by driveways and the tiniest of flowerbeds that clung precariously to the house. These flower beds contained the hollyhocks and other flowers planted by, I am sure, those long dead tenants and relatives. It was a heralding of the spring when mom would hang off the upstairs porch on a washday and call me to "come see aunt Lizzie's tulips and Aunt Marie's lilies." Come you must—it was just part of what you did. Unlike so many other families ours had a story for everything—every piece of furniture, every nook and cranny, every tenant family and even, I'll be darned, every tree and flower. Nothing just happened to be there.

We didn't use the front, front porch much (named because there was another front porch just off to the left). We did of course use both back porches—this was the way into the house. Occasionally we would use the front stairs but these occasions were few and far between. These stairs were very steep and led to our living room, which you will understand, was so crowded that to open the door was nearly impossible. In our house everyone came in the back door, company and all! You would wind around the cellar door, past the tenant's door, up the stairs, around the corner, through the outer door, into the tiny enclosed porch and knock on the door. There mom (or dad) would part the curtain to check on the caller before opening the door. The key to the door was one of those old, large brass keys that today you see in floral arrangements or as collector's items. I am sure when we left mom took the key even though the house was to be demolished and there would be no further need of it.

You entered the kitchen, a typical old Victorian kitchen with tin ceiling (how I hated having to wash it twice a year), old converted coal stove, and a crowding of appliances, furniture, washtubs and such. The stove was huge and took some taking care of. It originally had been a coal burner, converted later to a "modern" oil-burning stove. That meant we had a bottle of oil strategically placed on a stand behind the pantry door next to the refrigerator (known always in our house as the ice box).

When I think of it by today's standards it was such a fire hazard. We had to lug a five-gallon jug of oil from the cellar up two flights of stairs and carefully place it on a stand. There it dripped through a metal tube that snaked from the stand behind the refrigerator, under the window, over the washtubs, around the floor behind the washing machine, past the hot water heater to the stove where it finally dripped into an opening near the wall. I recall the smell and the trek to the cellar especially in the winter when the stairs would be slippery. To this day, I remember going into the darkened cellar convinced that just out of sight was that fiend who would attack me. I never outgrew that fear even as I became a teenager and young adult.

Behind the table was a bureau of some sort that was crowded with all kinds of things and above it a shelf that for all the years I lived there held my dead aunt's metal bank, a glass weather vane filled with blue water, Grandma Wallis's old loudly ticking clock and a box containing green stamps. This kitchen was the place of great meals, washday rituals, warm irons heating in the oven (to be carried to my attic bedroom), clothes draped over the oven and the shelf drying in the winter and of course our mittens hanging up to dry.

Just off to the right was the bathroom, a tiny narrow room with just enough space for the claw foot bathtub and toilet, the old fashioned kind with a fancy pull chain. It had originally been part of the adjacent bedroom, made into the "water closet" by grandpa at the turn of the century. There was no sink—you had to brush your teeth, shave and attend to those activities at the kitchen sink located in the pantry while in full site of everyone. Mornings would be real family time. Dad would be shaving, mom would be cooking and preparing lunches and us kids would be eating, all within an arms length of each other.

Our dining room and living room were like every other room in the house, crowed with furniture. The dining room, probably about 12' by 12' held the dining room table and chairs, buffet, china closet, desk, wind up Victrola, a trunk and of course the "furnace" which was really a large, black upright pot bellied stove. Now that did not leave much room for getting around. But somehow we all managed to gather friends and family time and time again.

One Easter my brother decided to borrow some Easter rabbits and there they were in their hutches for all to see and smell while we ate our Easter dinner. On occasions of heavy rain, black soot and water would run down the wall from the stove pipe opening and us kids were called into duty to bring the old newspapers and rags and station ourselves strategically to make sure it never got onto the rug or traveled further than the dining room. We were supposed to head off this running river of blackness, however, there were times when my brother and I just happened to let it flow freely to see just how far it would travel.

Located just off the dining room was a screened in porch that provided shade and a place for summer meals. Mom would serve the dinner and we would talk of pretty places while looking across the street at the railroad yards. We would sometimes use candles, fancy dishes and glasses, and always, absolutely always a clean starched tablecloth. When we finished eating we would trek everything back indoors. You could not leave too much out there as everything became dusted with soot from passing trains and exhaust from passing cars and trucks.

The living room, ah the parlor! It was certainly not fancy and unlike so many people who do not use their living room but rather keep it for show, our living room was just that—a place to live in. Here too was a conglomeration of furniture most of which came to us by way of someone else. There was an upright piano that held the famous dog statues and hanging glass fragile thing that was again grandma's. All the time I lived in the house I never, not once heard anyone play that piano. When we left the house it remained behind either to be razed along with the house or to be taken by vandals who rummaged the soon to be demolished homes along the street.

The living room, always referred to as the parlor, contained as you might guess, an assortment of furniture. At one time mom and dad slept in there in a double bed placed in front of the piano. That was when grandma was still alive. Imagine if you can, a room filled with furniture and at Christmas the biggest tree you could imagine, reaching to the ceiling and branching out to touch you as you climbed into or out of the bed. When Aunt Lizzie and Uncle Jack sold their house and moved away for a while, mom volunteered to take care of their furniture till they returned.

Now placed into this already over crowed living room was more furniture and in center stage (the double bed was gone by now) a large Roseville two-piece jardinière with this huge palm tree. Well where do you think it landed? Yep, right in the middle of the room. You looked over it, around it or through it for months and months. Howdy Doody and The Lone Ranger had very real scenery.

By today's standards for a "typical" home, ours was one of moderation. Rooms were not oversized, and you had to move from room to room by passing through a room. No welcoming large entrance halls, no contemporary family room. There were the usual additions of scrolled decoration found on Victorian homes.

The basement, as the house itself was loaded with stuff. There were unusual items such as the sand bins (still holding sand) that Grandpa used to store apples and potatoes all winter. There was an old raccoon coat hanging and furniture and just about any thing else your vivid imagination could conger up. I left the house as a very young lady who was dying to just have new things around me. I am sure we left a treasure trove of antiques and collectables in that cellar when, at last, with every bit of strength left, we closed the door forever leaving behind memories tangible and intangible. We had taken so much; we had left behind so much. Our new home was not as big and already almost full with our booty.

In a time far from now will someone feel the same about our new house? I doubt it. Our newer home is located in a more suburban contemporary neighborhood. My parents are still living there and have been for almost forty years. There are memories here too but these more modern memories cannot match those stemming from our gray clapboard house. That one held generation after generation, story after story.

But who is to say that someday perhaps a new generation will delve through closets and cellar and hold up something and wonder about its origin. Maybe the same words will be used and the same feelings generated. Impossible, maybe not.

Under The Eaves

Under The Eaves

I love attics. Even today if I go into an attic I feel at home and comfortable. Not long ago a friend of mine asked me if I would mind helping her clean out her uncle's attic as he had been moved to a rest home and would not likely return. I followed her up the stairs to the second floor, then climbed the dark, dank attic stairs until I came upon the space under the eaves. Nestled among the years of accumulated objects, I could just imagine all the treasures just lying there waiting to be found.

You see, I grew up in an attic. Well, I didn't spend all my time there but enough of it to have it make a lasting impression. Now if you told someone today that you slept in the attic that had no heat in the winter and was so hot in the summer you could hardly breathe, they would immediately assume you had been the victim of poverty. Hardly the case, that's just the way it was back then and there are many people who can attest to that. Personally, I thought it was wonderful. There I was all alone in my castle turret, my special place in the world where I could look out of the third floor window across the railroad tracks and watch the city lights at night and the sun shining on all of the homes across town during the day.

From my window I could see across the street to Jackson's Stone Yard where mom would spend hours as a child climbing on the rocks and boulders. In later years it became a lumber company, however, the boulders and rocks remained in piles and before the high fence went up, I too climbed on those rocks whose stories of long ago came to life.

To get to our attic you had to go through my parents bedroom then climb the dark cluttered stairs into the middle room, then turn left at the top into my bedroom. I choose that room because it had one of the only windows in the attic and was the least cluttered of the three. The other two rooms contained a lifetime of treasures from assorted relatives both living and dead. Since my mom had assumed the role of caretaker of family memorabilia, and the house had been home to these assorted relatives you can just imagine what riches were to be found there.

You may not believe this but we were the proud owners of everything from the regular family photo albums, unused furniture, outgrown clothes, Christmas ornaments right down to the most unusual items that included my deceased grandfather's wooden leg and my uncle's appendix that was kept in a jar. I would delight kids on the way to school with stories of these gross things that I had and they did not. There was also this metal gadget that looked like a skeleton of a Quonset hut. It was about four feet long and about three feet wide and had been used to protect my grandfather's damaged leg which later was amputated (thus the wooden leg). I would place a square piece of cloth over it and use it as a house for dolls, my brother on the other hand would use it as a railroad tunnel.

There was also a tarnished silver memorial cup with an inscription to someone unknown that I would use when I dressed up in my princess outfits. I was convinced that this was the royal trophy that had been in the family for years and had been presented to us by the King of England. The inscription was meaningless and yet represented just another opportunity for a little girl to play make believe. To this day I never found out exactly where it came from or to whom the inscription was dedicated.

Years ago these three attic rooms had been honest to goodness bedrooms beautifully decorated with wallpaper and hardwood floors. The faded scenes on the paper dimly showed lilies in fields somewhere in the county. There was a chimney in the middle room and antique gas light fixtures that had been converted to electricity. These rooms had been bedrooms to those assorted relatives from long ago. Now except for my room, they were totally filled with memories both tangible and intangible.

When I was little, I would sometimes imagine that some of these objects took on a life of their own and often mom would be summoned to calm the fears of a child with an overactive imagination. She would climb the stairs and snuggle next to me in bed relating stories when she too occupied an attic room.

Most of the time it was quite comfortable up there in spite of lack of heat in winter or a fan in the summer. However, there were extremes. In the putrid summer days, it was so hot that I could only lie on the linoleum that covered the floor. There I would roll from spot to spot as the floor heated below my body and I rolled to the next cool spot. I don't recall feeling that the floor was hard, just nice and cool. I would fall asleep near the window and wake up clear across the room after rolling and rolling all through the night.

Winter was a totally different picture. Mom would place an old flat iron in the oven of our big kitchen stove and then wrap it in a towel for me to carry up to the bed. I would place it in just the right spot, then get in wearing my winter sleeping garb. This consisted of underwear, flannel pajamas, socks, sweater, hat, mittens and scarf. I also had the added weight of about four blankets. Once in the bed you made no effort to remove yourself from this winter den. Luckily I was young and did not (as one grows older) need to remove myself to use the bathroom. In the morning, you could not see out of the window because of the frost (on the inside) but you could make scratched ice pictures that you hoped would stay there till you returned home from school.

In the spring, the Rose of Sharon tree whose branches reached over the porch roof would provide me with pretty flowers to see. I was very tempted to see if I could reach out and pick one but caution prevented me from such activity since I would have had to hang by my feet from the window sill and lie across the sloping roof.

Most of the time the attic proved to be a safe heaven for a little girl. There were no monsters and I never had to share a room with anyone. It was all mine. There was one time though when I was awakened by a frantic call from a stranger. I awoke to see my room lit by flames that were exploding from the lumber company building across the street. Quickly we grabbed what we could find and fled down the street wearing only our night clothes. Mom took the two Staffashire dogs from England and two empty suitcases. There we stood in the cold night air watching to see if our home was to be destroyed. The firefighters sprayed water on it all night and when it was over and we were allowed to return, we dashed to the attic to view the damage across the street. There we sat huddled together grateful for the blessing of our home.

As I grew older, the composition of my room changed. I put away my dolls and childhood toys and decorated the room as one might expect of a young lady. Aunt Lizzie had given me an old dressing table and in place of dolls and games, I had more and more books. I had a doilies and a lace bedspread from Aunt Marie. Hanging on the dressing table were the beginnings of womanhood, earrings, necklaces and of course the gloves.

When we moved from the house, I was much older and not at all interested in taking all the possessions. We were moving to a newer house that had an empty attic and basement and was all on one floor and to me that was heaven. Looking back now I am sorry that I did not take more items with me. I can only imagine the treasures that were left behind, first for the looters who pillaged the house and then finally to be destroyed forever by the wrecking ball that demolished the house and removed any traces of its existence.

Inside all of those boxes were the accumulations of generations of family who came from far away, began new lives in a new country and now were no longer.

As the years passed and I had children of my own, I always wanted to own another "attic" home. I would have liked my children to experience the wonderful feeling of having a special place far removed from the rest of the house with treasures to explore and stories to make up. Someday perhaps even as age settles in and the "flight to fancy" might take a wee bit longer, I intend to have an attic bedroom. This time it will be warmed by furnace heat, have air conditioning in summer, and maybe, just maybe a Rose of Sharon tree outside of the window.

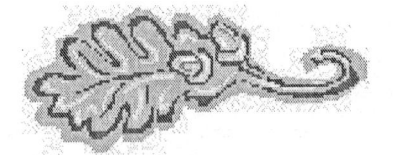

Duggan School

Duggan School

Duggan School was located within walking distance from my home on South Leonard Street. It was a large red brick, two story structure with a combination clock and bell tower in the front, and in the back the school yard surrounded by a high black wrought iron fence. The school took up most of a city block and had been the neighborhood school for many years. Had it been built when mom was younger, she would have attended it also, but her elementary days were spent in a much smaller building closer to her home.

The school was an impressive structure especially for a little girl about to enter kindergarten. I remember mom holding my hand as we approached the stairway leading to the classrooms. I held on tightly as we neared the room that would be my first ever classroom. The kindergarten room, overseen by a Miss Noonan, held an array of wooden toys and things usually associated with the first year of school. My fondest recollection was of a large, homemade white two story doll house with tiny curtains at the windows and a wooden family just waiting to be brought alive. Whenever possible I would escape to the doll area and play all sorts of make believe either alone or in the company of other like-minded girls and maybe a few boys.

The classroom had very high ceilings and long, narrow windows with shades that, if you pulled the correct cord went both up on the top and down on the bottom. It was important to make sure the shades hung correctly in each room so that the windows looked uniform throughout the school and attractive from the outside. Because children were allowed to write and make pictures on the chalk boards, the room always smelled of chalk dust. I can remember watching the tiniest of particles floating in the sunshine as the children erased a picture or a word. To some children I think the erasing part was what they enjoyed most. Older children were allowed to go outdoors just before dismissal to "clap the erasers." This was an assigned task and one that youngsters looked forward to doing.

Mine was a half day kindergarten—I walked all the way from home in the morning and back home in the afternoon, a distance of about a half mile. Whether I was in the company of others I do not recall but looking back I am sure mothers of today would not allow such a journey. Gram was bedridden and mom was unable to walk with us.

A few years ago while cleaning out a box from the cellar mom showed me a picture of myself that had appeared in the local newspaper. I do not recall why the entire kindergarten class had been featured on the front page, I only know that there I was in my baloney curls squatting down in front, dress hiked up enough to now be embarrassing. In those days all girls wore dresses or jumpers or skirts and blouses. It was not until the school years of my children that pants became the norm for both boys and girls.

Duggan housed students from kindergarten through eighth grade with additional rooms assigned to the principal, office staff and the nurse. There was no lunchroom, there was however a large gymnasium/auditorium and an enclosed pool.

My days at Duggan were the happy days of childhood, a time to explore new adventures and relationships. There were no big yellow buses carrying us to school. Everyone walked. You were up at the crack of dawn, given a good breakfast and sent along your way in time to make the bell. We did not carry backpacks or lunch boxes. If we needed to carry something it was placed into a brown sack.

Weather was just something you dealt with. In the winter I wore union suits and boots known as "Arctic's." A union suit, much to my dismay, was a one piece, white heavy cotton garment fashioned with buttons down the front and a "trap door" in the bottom. It was warm alright but oh so embarrassing. Thank God mom allowed me to wear rayon panties over the bottom of it so I could continue to feel like a little girl.

I was to remain in Duggan for all of my elementary school years. Some recollections are easy like the time Miss Brady told me to hold out my hand as though making a fist. I had done something wrong, although I am not sure what, but whatever it was I needed a good "rapping" on the knuckles with the ruler. I remember the time also when we were lined up to go to the nurses office to see if we had head lice. There you would take your turn sitting in a chair while the nurse shone a blue light onto your scalp. All us kids would stand around watching this and waiting for the word that some kid had to go home.

One time when the nurse had us all lined up, she was walking backwards to make sure we remained as placed, she fell backwards into a bucket of soapy water that the janitor was using to mop the corridor floor. How we laughed, how we were lectured! What a sight to see this young lady sitting in the bucket of suds soaking wet and trying not to cry as we howled in laughter.

Along the way to and from school there was time for many adventures. After all this was an urban school in the late 40's and early 50's and all sorts of establishments lined the streets of our route. There were city dwellings mostly two and three family homes and also wooden and brick tenements that housed many families. There were businesses of all sorts, shops, factories, churches, parks and the opportunity for adventure was everywhere. There were also characters of all sizes, shapes, ages and we, the lucky ones had this adventure all to ourselves.

Along the route we would see other children going to Duggan. Some (the very young ones) were accompanied by parents for a few days at the beginning of the school year but most walkers did so alone accompanied only by their friends or acquaintances. I am sure we were safe; in all those years I never heard of any thing happening to anyone other than the usual trouble kids get into. Shop keepers watched from their doorways and parents all along the way hollered to us to keep going, "don't stop your mother is waiting for you."

As we approached the upper grades our gym class included swimming. This was fine by me since I was a good swimmer and hated, positively hated regulation sports like baseball. I was not good at sports and dreaded the awful day when it was time to participate. You know when you get that feeling in your stomach that warns you of impending doom.

This girl named Rosemary loved to make fun of me when I swung for the ball and missed time after time. Today she would be called a "jock," in those days she was just the bane of my existence.

We had to wear uniforms for gym, dark blue shorts and blouses; mom said they looked just like hers. They had to be neatly starched and ironed and the gym teacher would walk down the row as though we were in a barracks ready for inspection. We were told it was part of our duty as young ladies to keep up our appearance, personally I think she wasn't all that fond of gym period either.

There were several routes to and from home and school. Most of the time we just stuck with the regular one but sometimes when we felt adventurous we would deviate a little. One route took us by a poultry store where live chickens were displayed in wooden crates in the window. You could hear it and smell it long before you passed by it's chicken feathered windows. Emanating from the back of the store were the noises that I learned later were from chickens held by the feet while shown to customers. I didn't dare ask how these live hens were readied for the trip home.

Another shop was the wonderfully smelling leather shoe repair shop of an Italian gentleman. He was related to our tenants and although he had a proper name everyone called him the cobbler. This shop was frequented when the soles of our shoes would wear out or our buckles came off of our Arctic's. Even though the charge for his services was minimal we kept our shoes until the very last minute when it was evident that we could not get our feet into them one more time.

Across the street from Duggan was the local drugstore, Kenausis Drugs, complete with a soda fountain. We would, if time and money allowed, sit up on a stool and ask for a vanilla or cherry Coke. This establishment had it's own smell. It was a combination of vitamins and soda fountain treats. There were times when mom would bring us kids into the drugstore and ask for advice from the druggist. Nothing was out of bounds. She would hike up my skirt a just a little or unbutton the sleeves on my blouse to ask his advice about a rash.

Prescriptions were sent home in tiny boxes or glass bottles of different colors and sizes. I am sure the tiny boxes are still at moms and I would venture to say the glass bottles are there too. Because we did not have a lot of money Mr. Kenausis would loan us such things as vaporizers. Mom had been instructed that these were a lot more effective for a little girl with croup than the creosol lamp she burned in my room.

One or two days a week the city library branch would be open. It stood across the street and a little way from the school. Oh what happiness when I could go there to take out books! I remember a series about children from other cultures and other times. There was one about a family in the Ice Age. The library was frequented by neighbors and teachers alike.

In the other direction was St. Patrick's, a large gothic style church with a huge rectory on the side. I was told that God himself lived there and you could see him if you looked very carefully. I wasn't sure I wanted to run into him. One day we quietly entered, blessed ourselves with cold, cloudy water and approached the sanctuary with guarded steps. My friend decided to kneel in front of the candle holder to say a special prayer. She took out a coin and put it into the coin box. It jingled on the way down. She told me that you could only say a prayer if you paid for it. I thought I had better do the same. As hard as I looked I could not find a coin but I did find two candy corns covered with pocket lint.

Very carefully I placed them into the coin box and listened as they jingled on their way down. I was convinced that this offering was good enough to allow me to say a prayer. After all, if God himself was really around he might appreciate such a treat.

The neighborhood also had a beer brewery that you could smell from some distance. We were instructed never to stop by there and in fact we told mom that we never walked that route but we really did. There were casks lined up on loading docks and men moving them onto trucks. Coming around the corner onto Porter

Street brought us smack dab by a funeral home. This was the place to be extremely cautious because the older kids would make up gruesome stories about what happened in there and what would happen to us if we were not careful.

Duggan was my foundation for education and my beginning place to move from childhood to adulthood. It still stands as it always did however today it is used as a school for special needs children. It is not often that I am in the neighborhood, nor often that I think of those days. Today I am busy with grandchildren who go to school on a big, yellow school bus. They have never clapped erasers nor worn union suits. They have no idea what they are missing.

Sulfur Powder

Sulfur Powder

When I was a child and sick, I was kept in my parent's bedroom. This tiny room was just off the dining room and close enough to the kitchen so mom could keep an eye on me while she went about her daily chores. Normally I slept in the attic but when I was sick I had the special privilege of the "big bed" and along with the "big bed" came special activities geared to keeping one rambunctious little girl in tow.

Mom would allow such activities that normally you would not think of doing when assigned to bed. One was making tents. She would bring in dad's big old black umbrella and shore it up somehow, and then I was allowed to drape the sheet over it and climb into this special hiding place. One time my brother and I had to share the bed as we both had chicken pox and in those days that automatically meant "off to bed." We must have been a sight with all those spots and calamine lotion dabbed on our skin. Every so often mom would yell from the kitchen, "no scratching."

We would have contests to see who could jump the highest and touch the ceiling, or on warm days hang the furthest out of the second story window. Of course none of this was done within earshot of mom. Once my brother and I climbed out onto the porch roof and sat there in our night clothes watching the other kids walk home from school. The roof was pitched and we were mighty careful not to venture too close to the edge.

Mom would spend lots of time with us when we were sick; time she managed to find in between her duties of housework and caring for grandma, dad and the kids. She wasn't one to fuss about keeping things in order or adamant about messes or the lack of. If we were happily playing and out of mischief for a while all activities were tolerated. Empty boxes were artistically made into play stoves and cradles. Crayons and paints, home made play dough and arts and craft materials found their way into the bedroom. Dolls also became "sick" and the same lavish attention paid to me was paid to them.

Doll pills, lotions, potions and bandages were just the thing to keep a sick doll from distress as much as to keep a sick little girl from boredom. My dolls came down with all the ailments of childhood including some made up ones that required additional (M and M) pills or extra doses of ice cream.

This to unbelievably was the time of the house call. Yes that's right the doctor actually came to your home to examine patients, prescribe medications and talk at length with folks. Dr. C was our family physician. He was by all standards the expert on everything and anything that ailed you. To this day over fifty years later mom still harkens back to what Dr. C would do or say. He was the expert! There was never a decision to get a second opinion nor to doubt his word.

Mom would call the doctor's number, often getting his wife on the phone. After a brief explanation a time was scheduled for the house call.

In anticipation of this important visit, hands and faces were scrubbed, clean "jammies" would be put on and the kettle was placed on the stove for a cup of tea. Oftentimes the doctor would examine more than the patient. If the doctor was coming we would line up and mom would tell him what she was concerned about and he would take a look at all of us. Same price!

On these occasions even the neighbors would be included. Our tenants would come up to see if there was anything they could do. The next door neighbors would holler over the porch railings to mom to offer their advice. Stories were exchanged, and remedies shared. Nothing, not even sickness was private. It seemed like everyone got in on the act.

When the doctor finally arrived mom would greet him with all the warmth of a relative. She would lead him into the bedroom and I would be examined. The doctor would also take time to ask about my doll(s) and offer advice for their well being. If anyone else was around they too would be paraded out and examined if necessary. A visit to Grammy's room would definitely be in order. Then Dr. C would sit for a few minutes and enjoy a hot cup of tea and perhaps fresh homemade cookies.

This was the time of no antibiotics. This was the time when we were given sulfur powder. This white sulfur powder, the magic potion would have to be mixed with juice to enable one to swallow it. For years I never had Welch's Grape Juice except with sulfur powder mixed into it. It was the juice that mom kept for just such occasions. Although try as she may, the white powder usually floated on the top of the juice and would taste horrible on the way down. This powder came from our neighborhood drug store and oftentimes would be delivered to our door. Mom, true to her mission in life to not throw away anything useful, still has tiny cardboard boxes from the drug store labeled, "Sulfur Powder, take as directed."

Antibiotics and new treatments of all sorts have done much to alleviate pain and suffering and diminish time spent in bed. Today's families with both parents working leaves little time with sick children for tent making, box decorating, house calls by physicians or Welch's Grape Juice with sulfur powder. Now I buy Welch's Grape Juice just because it is good for you and I have acquired a taste sans the added medicine. However, once in a while, if I think about it I can look into the glass and see for a brief second the white powder floating on top and almost expect to taste once again the special concoction from mom.

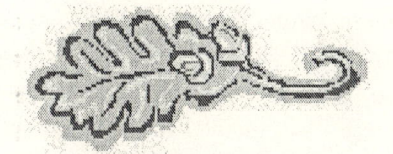

Baloney Curls

Baloney Curls

You don't often hear about baloney curls anymore, you know the ones found on America's sweetheart Shirley Temple. I also had baloney curls. Many a picture of my younger days from toddler to little girl show me with baloney curls tumbling from my head, reaching down to my shoulders, oftentimes with a bow decorating my locks. It was a daily ritual for me to stand in front of mom as she brushed and brushed and brushed some more and then very carefully, using one finger and the brush would twirl the hair around and around the finger making one baloney curl after another.

I guess in a way I was lucky. I did have lovely curls. Mom said people would stop and comment on how pretty the baloney curls looked. However, as I grew up I became less interested in standing for long periods of time while enduring the brushing and twirling. I also became less interested in baloney curls. As I grew in age my concern became more about a grown up mature look—probably when I entered what would be called the middle grades—I was determined to cut the curls and perhaps try one of the latest hairstyles, a pageboy.

To accomplish this I needed to have straighter hair, baloney curls would no longer do. So morning after morning I stood alone in front of the mirror and tried every which way to get the correct look. Try as I may it never looked quite like the pictures I saw in magazines or on the TV screen. When at last I could no longer stand the hairdo I asked my girlfriend if her mom would cut my hair. This was my friend who lived on a block up the street and whose mom had been a hair dresser.

On that fateful day I took my dollar bill and made my way to their apartment. My friend's mom did a nice job and I returned home with a short haircut that was easy to take care of. Gone were the baloney curls for good!

These were not the days of hairspray, mousse or holding gel. These were not even the days of a hand-held hairdryer that blew warm air and kind of gave some fullness and body to the hair. We did have a funny looking hairdryer that had been my mom's. Like so many other things it was found in the attic and looked more like a contraption to remove paint from the side of a building. There were rows of electric coils that would become red as the dryer became hotter. It was both a nuisance and a hazard. In our house wet hair was just dried with a towel or in warmer weather, the sun.

Trips to the beauty parlor were few and far between. In fact, I think I only went once or twice during all of my high school and college days. To my recollection mom never went to a beauty parlor in all the years I have known her. She still wears her hair up in bun, the golden locks now a silver gray. I remember thinking how nice it would be to have a mom who did go to the beauty parlor and wore her hair like my friend's mom. But there was always something about her that lent itself to a bun on the back of her head.

Most of the time I was content with my hair and wore the same short look from early adolescence until many years later when an event happened that would become a concern for me. It was when our first grandchild was born and I looked at the pictures of myself standing at the bedside of my daughter who was holding the new baby. "Who is that old lady?" I asked myself. "How did my hair get to be so gray so fast?" For a few moments while looking at the photos I think I became more interested, at least it seemed that way, in this gray headed lady than I did with the babe in arms. Good God, how did it happen?

A few days later I promptly called a beauty parlor and scheduled an appointment. I brought along a picture of a younger me when the hair on my head was brown, my brown! The hairdresser and I chose a color as close to the picture as possible and the dying began. When I left the salon I felt like a new woman, well maybe not new but at least a little younger.

I received compliments from young and old alike. They came from co-workers, friends, children and neighbors. I was young again, or so I thought. The magic of chemicals! For almost 11 years I dyed my hair. It was a "not so pleasant" event and I waited for as long as I could to do the deed. Usually it was done on a Sunday evening just before a good movie on TV. I would drape myself with old, stained towels and mix up the potion. Then onto the head it would go. An hour later I was done, shampooed and styled.

Well, time again has gone by. As I approach another stage in my life I have decided to become more aware of health issues one of which is the chemicals used in hair dye. So again I made a decision. This time a "biggy." I would let my hair grow out to it's now natural color of gray. It took a while. There were periods when I had job interviews and felt the need to color my hair. My God, I thought what would potential employers think of this gray-haired lady? Then I didn't care. If I was to have an interview I would go exactly as myself, assured, mature, and even beginning to enjoy the "real me."

The South Leonard Street Bus

The South Leonard Street Bus

Passing by our house was a green and yellow "chariot" that made numerous runs throughout the day and evening. This chariot offered the riders opportunities galore and for a little girl beginning to explore the world, an opportunity for adventure. The "chariot" had a driver and he was the individual who, once we paid our fare, took us on these adventures. Now of course he was not a tour director and our destinations were not as glamorous as those you read about in the Travel Section of the Sunday paper, nonetheless these outings had all of the ingredients to delight this little traveler.

The South Leonard Street bus played an important role in our lives and the bus was a primary source of transportation during those years. It ran right by our gray two family Victorian house at 222 South Leonard Street and stopped almost right in front of the house on the way home and across the street when we took it to go somewhere.

It was quite thrilling to "catch" the bus and I recall those times quite vividly. My first memories of the bus were the ones that had to do with my dad. He took the morning bus to work and the evening bus home. Folks today would call it commuting. We just called it "catching the bus."

In the morning, Mom would prepare his lunch while he washed and shaved in the pantry just off the kitchen. I don't recall there was much privacy then as our bathroom, also located just off the kitchen, did not have a sink so anyone who had to "wash up" did it in the panty. There was no door and because it was also the storage room for kitchen supplies you were forever being bumped by those reaching for things. There you were washing, shaving and brushing your teeth while folks in the kitchen went about their business. Contrary to contemporary life whose family members all have their own well appointed bathrooms, this setup lent itself ideally to family "quality time."

When it got to be a quarter to eight, dad would grab his lunch and head out to the bus, lunch pail in hand and a red thermos of freshly made coffee. He would hug and kiss mom and us kids. Mom would run to the living room and wait in the window till the bus came down the street. In warmer weather she would open the window and hang out waving to those walking by or waiting for the bus. Since we lived on the second floor the figure of this mistress of the manor could be seen up and down the street.

It was a routine and she never ever missed the "good-bye's." In later years she would even hang out the window waving a white handkerchief to flag down the bus if one of us were running late and the bus just had to wait. Frankly I was embarrassed by her behavior when she did this and mad at the person who had the gall to cause this action. Usually, in fact almost always it was my brother. He was perpetually late and often ended up running down the street after the bus to grab it at the next stop.

At night this chariot brought dad home and many an evening I would run down the stairs to meet him and get the first hug as he disembarked from the bus. He would wave to those left on board then turn to hold my hand as we trudged up the driveway and headed up the stairs. "How's my chicken tonight?," he would ask.

It was totally unheard of to travel in what would be referred to today as casual clothes. Perish the thought! When you took the bus you had to dress up just as though you were off to church or school or on a Sunday visit. Hats and gloves were not optional, they were the appropriate dress. Tucked away in a drawer even today are gloves that were worn back then.

One vivid adventure comes to mind every December, our annual Christmas shopping expedition. Mom and I would dress as though we were off on a Himalayan trek, empty bags in hand to cart home our loot. We would wait across the street, often after school when the day was fading and there was a definite time limit to get as much stuff as time and strength allowed.

The bus would be full of holiday shoppers old and young,

some babies in tow and others so old they could hardly climb the three stairs to get onboard. An excitement filled the air and conversations traveled back and forth from seat to seat, generation to generation and ethnic background to ethnic background gradually filling the bus with more and more voices as more and more travelers came aboard. These were the people of your life, the ones you saw each and every day. They knew your family and you knew theirs and so there you rode on into the waning daylight hours through city streets, over bumps and ruts and patches of ice laughing and talking and sharing the great adventure.

As we approached downtown the excitement built. There were the stores whose windows were filled with every imaginable gift just waiting to be bought and I pressed my face to the window wiping the frosted glass with my gloved hand to be sure I did not miss anything. The streets had garlands stretched across from pole to pole and when we arrived at the green, the tree was ablaze with thousands and thousands of lights. Fifth Avenue and Macys's were not even in the running!

On the way home our bundles carefully placed by our feet and in our laps, mom and I would make plans for the gift wrapping that was to come. There was no FM radio blaring the latest top 10 songs, no CD humming a tune, no seat belts to put on, no adjustable seats that warmed themselves at the touch of a button. There was just us on this wonderful chariot ride, mom and me on an adventure.

My recollections include the ride that would change my life forever. It was the ride with mom to show me the way to the Girl's Club located just off the downtown area. I was to go there once a week to take sewing lessons. Finally the great day arrived. I was allowed to take the South Leonard Street bus all by myself. Imagine that, traveling through city streets with strangers dressed in Sunday best off to an adventure of my very own. No ride anywhere has had such significance. After that it seemed that I—me, myself and I could climb on board, drop the change or token into the box, wait for the ching, ching sound as the money giggled down and then take my seat. I could just imagine the driver saying to me, "Your chariot awaits my dear, won't you step on board."

Winter Wash Day

Winter Wash Day

(Or Standing At Attention)

Washday at our house was Thursday, certainly not in keeping with the popular nursery rhyme that led one to believe that Monday alone was set aside for just that chore. No, in our house it was Thursday. This major production would begin right after breakfast and last well into the late afternoon.

The great white ringer washer was rolled out closer to the wash tubs. The old black rubber hose used to fill it was removed from the interior and threaded across the room over chairs and door knobs and finally attached to the pantry faucet well across the room. Once the tap was turned on and the flow began, woe to anyone who happened by and bumped the hose. More than once water streamed onto the floor accompanied by the screams of those who either caused it to happen or felt the cool wet liquid upon their feet.

When the washer was filled, the hose was moved to the washtubs, two side by side huge black stone tubs set on legs in the corner of the kitchen. These tubs had white painted metal tops that held all kinds of things during the week, including more than once a sick child whose bed was made on top of the washtubs so mom could keep an eye on them. On wash days these covers were tilted up and rested on the wall. There they remained unless of course, you happened to be the recipient of a good old bang on the head and shoulders if the lid slipped while you bent over the tubs shaking the clothes and moving them around in the rinse water.

Mom had a routine for all this activity and although she was never in the military, I felt sure she had in some way attended military training on the correct way to do laundry or at least was schooled on laundry doing somewhere before we arrived on the scene. If we children happened by, she would continue the weekly instruction on just how the scenario went. Woe to the one who deviated from the norm!

Clothes moved in logical rotation from the floor, whites first, to the washing machine, then through the wringer to the first wash tub of rinse water. Then finally to the last rinse water that contained just the correct amount of bluing. While this was going on, the next load usually medium colors hit the washer and the activity was repeated over and over again until all the clothes were done.

When the first load of whites came out, they were dumped on the oilcloth on the kitchen table for sorting. God forbid that clothes were not properly sorted and readied for the unveiling which now took place in sight of all the neighbors. Mom would hang off the porch and place them on the line. "Never droop anything," I was instructed. "Always make sure the seams are even, the clothes stretched properly so there will be less wrinkles." And of course, the big one . . . ."what would the neighbors say if the clothes did not look just right?"

In our neighborhood everyone's backyard and porch opened to a common area. From our porch on the second floor one could see the clothes line of just about everyone on the block. It was not uncommon to yell across from neighbor to neighbor, porch to porch and discuss laundry. "Looks like a good drying day today." "Mrs. Smith must still be sick, saw John hanging today." Or the worst remark of all. "Looks like the whites could have had a bit more going around."

Unlike today's laundry routine where you just place the load first in the washer, then quickly into the adjacent dryer, mom's routine continued to take up most of the day. There was line after line after line of clothes. While the loads washed and soaked and rinsed, she would run back and forth from porch to kitchen bringing in the dry ones and carrying out the wet ones.

If all this washing, running, grabbing, sorting, carrying

hanging, pulling was not enough, the equipment had to be returned to its rightful place. The water was drained by hand, the tubs and wringer machine were thoroughly wiped out, the baskets and clothespins brought in and of course, the folding began. Huge piles of clothes were everywhere. And that was in the good weather.

Now winter proved to be much more challenging. There was no dryer and no cellar empty enough or close enough to hang lines. Winter laundry days meant mom would don her warmest hat, coat, mittens and brush the snow and ice off the porch and head outside to hang the wash. Contemporary families have no idea what in God's name that could be like. As quickly as mom would hang out shirts and pants, jackets and underwear, nature would step in and turn them into stiff forms and figures that seemed to be hanging onto the line for dear life. There was no flapping in the wind, rather they seemed to take on a lifelike quality all their own. There they would be men, women, children all hanging on for dear life stiff as boards and just defiant against the wind.

Upon removal from the line, they would be carried into the house stiff as a board tucked vertically under her arm and looking somewhat like an angry child who was to be carted off to the bedroom to finish his tantrum. You could literally stand them up row upon row in the basket. Sometimes I would stand them at attention against the kitchen wall and pretend they were characters on stage in a play.

Winter days meant clothes here, there and everywhere. Certainly they did not dry outside, no, it was just to get them "sort of dry" so you could then drape these lifeless characters over chair backs, tubs, stoves, bathtubs and just about any surface that would hold them.

Usually I was glad when Thursday ended. Friday only meant the ironing board would be out for the day. This leg-less wooden structure would be balanced from the table to the washtub. Not to worry, if you bumped it at least your feet remained dry.

Drying Mittens

Drying Mittens

When you think of winter in New England you conjure up scenes of country roads, stone walls covered with snow, quaint villages, old barns reflecting long evening shadows across snow covered baron fields. My reflections of childhood in the winter were of city streets waiting for the scraping sound of the big plow, sidewalks that forever seemed to need shoveling and cold walks to school in the morning, home for noon lunch, back to school and home again in the afternoon. However, after all this activity was always time for sledding.

Now one might question where a city girl could go sledding. Question no further. In our neighborhood were many locations where you could drag your sled, push off and enjoy the thrill of "downhill." Our home, located squarely between 4th Street and 5th Street and across the street from the railroad yards provided ample opportunity for just such endeavors.

We would race home, change into our play clothes and off we were. This changing routine took place in our crowded old kitchen. Mom would have our wool snow suits, wool sweaters, wool scarves, wool hats, wool wristlets and woolen mittens hanging on our chair. Once dressed we'd hurry down the stairs, grab our sleds and off we'd go dragging them behind us carefully hitting all the snow patches along the sidewalks. One did not enjoy the sound of the runners on a bare sidewalk and the main street we lived on was out of bounds (at least until we were out of site of mom).

Fourth Street was OK but 5th Street was the favorite and drew us to its icy challenge. This huge city hill with three, four and six family houses on each side offered opportunity galore for dodging parked cars, pedestrians, fire hydrants, dogs and other sledders. The climb to the top was quite challenging and even at such an early age I do recall being winded somewhat when we'd reached the "summit."

Once there we'd position ourselves on the sled, grab the front steering bars, shove off and plow dangerously downhill. It matched everything these modern day Olympic down hillers do as far as obstacles. At least these modern down hillers have stationary obstacles. The Fifth Street downhill course oftentimes included objects, not always inanimate that could at anytime move into our path. We'd whiz by homeowners and renters who could only shake their heads in disbelief. Reaching the bottom of the hill could prove to be even more challenging. You see Fifth Street ran smack into Charles Street, another city street, not quite as busy as our main street but non the less one to be reckoned with. Cars would whiz by and unless we had lookouts stationed at the bottom of the hill, we would desperately try dragging our feet as we approached this dangerous intersection. There is a God or Guardian Angels because never, not once, was there an accident.

Holding our breath we'd continue past the intersection to the rest of Fifth Street and come to a stop right before the next busy street, our own main street. We would head for a snow bank where we would plow into the pile. The impact sent snow crystals flying upwards to sting our already frozen faces. This routine would be repeated loosing and gaining other kids as they were called home for supper.

If the Fifth Street conditions on the slope were not conducive to a "good run," we'd head to a more rural setting, the "meadows" on the other side of the railroad tracks. The "meadows," so called because when Grandpa arrived from England to settle in our home, this area was open fields of wildflowers and the "hill" was covered with tangled weeds and grasses. Getting here meant crossing the main street again, dragging our sleds across the railroad tracks and carefully avoiding the contraptions associated with railroad yards.

This run, although less dangerous from cars and obstacles, was not to be reckoned with lightly. We were not to play anywhere near the tracks nor to engage in conversation with men from the railroad, some who held the dubious distinction of being called "Gandy Dancers."

As the hours wore on and the day darkened, we would trudge home dragging our sleds behind us each step a little harder as the distance to home shortened. We were not only dog tired, our snowsuits, hats, scarves and of course the mittens were heavy with the added weight of imbedded snow. Looking back I often wonder just how much weight we actually gained on these "runs." We'd park the sleds on the downstairs porch and head for the heat of the kitchen and a dry warm outfit. These were definitely not the days of Polartec and polyester.

In the kitchen hung a wooden rack that swung over the wash tubs and the floor next to the stove. Even now on cold snowy days I recall drying mittens, drippings falling on newspapers carefully placed on the floor below. All this water, all this smell of wet wool and all this clutter. No dryers, no mud rooms, no garage, just a crowded kitchen, a haven for a little girl who was just plum "tuckered out" from an Olympic sized run.

The Lake Cottage

The Lake Cottage

Growing up we were fortunate to have a cottage by a lake. How we would look forward to loading up the car on the last day of school and riding out to the lake. While everyone else in the neighborhood could only look forward to a steamy, uncomfortable summer in the city with sidewalks that held your footprint in the hot pavement, we could look forward to lots of grass, a cool porch with lake breezes and of course, the best part, swimming all day in the lake just steps from our living room.

Although the cottage was fully furnished and contained most of the essentials a family of four would require, there were always additions that had to be transported from city to country. Not withstanding the usual clothes and linens and some personal effects, we also transported huge items such as our trusty white horribly heavy wringer washing machine. This contraption along with the hoses had to be carried from the second floor, around the corner, down the steps, across another porch and finally loaded into the trunk of the Chevy. There it would remain for the trip across the city and into the country, finally reaching the kitchen of the cottage. For years, mom and dad would carry this heavy object themselves. I can't imagine now how they did it, but I guess when you are motivated and the end result is months in the country, you find the extra strength.

On wash days at the lake, mom would transport pail after pail of water from the dock to the house until at last the tub was full and the washing could begin. Who today could imagine such a thing?

Summer at the lake also meant gathering fireflies in jars at night. We would run helter-skelter through the moist grass, mason jars in hand trying to capture the most fireflies. We would watch them in the jars for a while then upon the advice of mom and dad, release them into the dark evening sky. Other assorted creatures would find their way into our hands and ultimately into jars, baskets and cardboard boxes. There would be snails, worms, salamanders, frogs, toads, and once a small snake that a neighbor kid put on our porch.

During our months in paradise we would have many visits from family and friends. The Fourth of July was especially a time for the gathering. Dad would haul out his old army stove and huge kettles and begin the day with a fresh pot of coffee for the early arrivals. One by one they would come. Some with food in assorted containers, salads, desserts, and cookies. In preparation for this annual event mom would spend time, hours and hours in the kitchen preparing goodies. These were the days of little refrigerator space, so most of the goodies would remain unfinished adding mayonnaise and dressing at the start of the feast.

The four holer would get an extra scrubbing, us kids would get an extra talking to. "Remember your manners. Play with all the children not just a few. Don't take anyone into the lake until you asked permission from their parents and NO creatures are to be selected for scaring anyone. Do I make myself clear?"

The lake property consisted of two houses; one smaller cottage right on the lake which had been a store many years before and one larger home in the rear with attached porches and sheds. Completing this family compound was the 4 holer outhouse and a large gray garage located way in the back near the blackberry field. The larger home was rented to a family from the same city and we used the smaller cottage, one just the right size for us and because it sat only steps from the lake we had the privilege (mom's words) of watching magnificent sun sets from our open porch.

Hitchcock Lake had been home to dad's family. His grandparents had purchased the property in the first decade of the 1900's as a refuge from the sweltering city and because they both longed for a place similar to their youth. Only a few darkened photos remain showing dad and these older members of his family.

Life on the lake in the 40's and 50's provided the setting for numerous adventures. There was the everyday swimming, the picking of blackberries from our patch, the weekly visits from the peddlers selling wonderful native fruit and vegetables, the fish man and of course, the ice cream man rumbling along with his white truck and tinkling bell. We seldom wore shoes although that could prove to be a mistake when stepping on the horse chestnuts that covered our backyard.

At the lake things were different. Not only did the little four room house and contents look vastly different from our Victorian two family house in the city, but everything else was different. The four holer was not only your bathroom but a place to hide where you were sure no one would care to look. You took your bath in the lake. You captured tiny frogs and bugs. You proudly showed any and all visitors just how far out you could swim. Poison Ivy was treated with a concoction from a special fern and water that dad boiled on the stove and then dabbed the liquid onto a very itchy little girl.

One time I remember when a leach attached itself to my brother in a not so nice place and I was scolded for trying to watch the removal of this creature while my brother howled. I remember too when mom found lice in my hair and I had a gasoline shampoo and then a dip into the lake with brown soap and a scrub brush.

One very special memory was waiting for my dad to come down the main road. I would stand on the neighbor's lawn eagerly looking up the hill, waiting for the black Chevy to come along. Dad would stop, I'd hop onto the running board and off we would go with dad's arm holding his little girl tightly around the middle. Mom would greet us with a fresh, starched and ironed apron, the kind that has become a collectable today.

A few years ago the "old" house had to be torn down. This was the larger one that had been rented to tenants. It was now completely uninhabitable and a danger to those who dared to open it's doors. Mom and dad arrived at the lake some time before the construction crew came to begin their demolition. I am sure they spent the few brief minutes alone talking about all of the memories and of those who had occupied the home. I arrived at the lake well after the house had been dismantled and the tangible evidence of it's existence carted away.

I found mom and dad sitting in the middle of the yard on chairs that had been left behind. Thinking that I should try to make light of the situation I quickly made a few humorous statements and took out the camera. I took a few "funny" pictures like one of dad with an old kettle on his head, asked if they needed anything and then left them to their memories.

The large house was gone now just like the four holer and all that remained was the open space where the "old" house as it was called had stood. The smaller house, closer to the lake remained and was to be used only on occasion.

Now there would be no large gatherings of family and friends only the weekly meeting of the quilting club on Wednesdays in July and August and the "once in a while" family visit for a quick swim in the lake. Now our days were spent in other places and other memories were beginning to be made. It became harder for dad and mom to travel to the lake. Less and less they loaded up the car to make the trip. In the last year of dad's life he did not go at all.

Today the lake property stands abandoned. Grass is uncut, weeds fill the flower beds, the garage has tumbled in upon itself, the blackberries are a tangle of brown bushes, there are few if any visitors. It is over. I am not as sad as I thought I would be. I am ready to let go. It was a fanciful place for a little girl. She is grown now and there is a new place that holds her heart. Perhaps someone else with a little girl will buy it, perhaps someone will swim in the lake and play in a tiny house. I hope so. But I am convinced it will never be the same. There will be no four holer, no peddlers, and no rides on a running board.

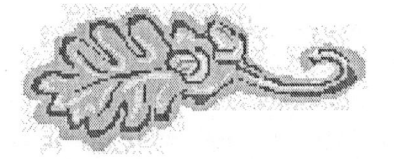

The Four Holer

The Four Holer

Growing up at the lake in the summertime meant using an outhouse. Ours was a particularly nice outhouse. I am sure the reader might not fully understand how anyone could call an outhouse "nice." But in fact, ours was probably the nicest one in the neighborhood. You see, our outhouse was a "four holer." That's right an outhouse with the convenience of having a hole just the right size for everyone and anyone who needed to use it.

The outhouse stood some distance from our cottage. It was located next to the garage, a distance that sometimes necessitated a run from the house or at least a quick walk.

It was painted white with tiny windows framed with green shutters. To the inexperienced with outhouses it looked sort of like a nice potting shed or tool shed. Surrounding the door step were wild tiny flowers of various shapes and sizes that lent a comfortableness to it. The door had a tiny window on the top and two windows, one on each side.

Stepping inside one knew instinctively that you were in an outhouse. It was spotless, receiving a daily scrubbing from mom, but those old outhouse users did not need to look around, your nose told you just where you were. Dad did his best to cart off the "stuff" and to lay in a supply of lime so as to alleviate as much as possible the bouquet.

We were quite proud of our four holer. Neighbors all had a common, smaller version with the standard one hole. I don't recall that any neighbor's outhouse even had tiny windows, shutters and lovely flowers complimenting the setting. This outhouse was used by our family for all of the years that I could remember. Then something happened. The four holer was sold. I can't quite remember just why but as with so many childhood memories, I can recall vividly when it was lifted onto a wagon and carried off. All in the neighborhood came to see it go and to my mind, bid it farewell. After that we used an outhouse like all the neighbors.

For some years the cottage was closed up and remained empty, no longer a family retreat from the sweltering city heat, no longer an imaginary world of make believe for a little girl. Gram had died and we were not to return to the lake for many years. The spot where the four holer had stood was overgrown with weeds and brambles. There was no trace of its regal splendor, its prominent location.

For years after that we spent summers in the city with the convenience of a real toilet, water tank above and pull chain dangling within arms reach. I often wondered just what became of the outhouse. It would have made a wonderful playhouse for a little girl and her dolls or a fort for the boys. Oftentimes my brother and I would use it as a hideout when playing hide and go seek with neighborhood pals or visiting cousins.

A few years ago a friend of ours gave us a book about outhouses in Alaska. There were big ones and small ones, fancy ones and unique ones but none of them could compare to our four holer. The book remains in our New Hampshire bathroom, the four holer remains in my memory.

The Virgin Mary

The Virgin Mary

When I was growing up I went to a small brick church up the hill from where we lived. It had been my mother's church and where my brother and I had been baptized. The congregation of this lovely church was rather small and oftentimes the services were sparsely attended but it was a warm, inviting place with a family atmosphere, the kind of church that lovingly took care of the parishioners in times of sickness or trouble.

To this day at age ninety-four mom still has a few remaining friends from her Sunday School class and a few mementoes of her growing years in the church. She tells wonderful stories of when the church had many members and had many social functions as well as Sunday services. There are pictures of her in plays that the members put on as well as certificates of achievement for milestones as a young member. This was where the Lucky Thirteen Club was founded, a group of Sunday School friends and their teacher who were to remain close friends for all of their adult lives.

The Rectory was located right next door and there the minister lived with his wife and family. Most of the time our ministers remained with the church for years and it was easy to consider them to be a friend as well as a spiritual leader. However, one minister and his family did leave after only a few years to become missionaries in the South Pacific. The children in the Sunday School learned much that year about missionary work and the location of the remote island that would be their home for three years. Upon their return, the minister came to a church picnic and told wonderful stories of his and his family's adventures on the island including how many of the church members wore grass skirts to the services.

This was where I first learned about church suppers, rummage sales, Christmas Bazaars, and the excitement of wearing my new Easter clothes and shoes. We would make our trip to Brown Brother's Store for the shoes and then on to Bank Street to buy the dress that I could hardly wait to put on. Everything had a special smell on Easter. New leather shoes, fancy clothes and of course the flowers that lined the alter. Mom would always make sure the names of deceased family members appeared in the bulletin and it was the tradition that the Easter lilies were for her parents and the tulips for her sisters.

It was here that we attended Sunday School, helped at the Christmas Bazaar, sang in the Junior Choir and hopefully learned about all those things that Sunday Schools teach children. I can honestly say that I was a much better student than my brother who time and again was escorted from the classroom for disruptive behavior. It was most embarrassing to a little girl and then a young lady when your brother continued to tease those sitting closest to him. I was convinced that although he attended church he was taking a lot of chances with God. He didn't seem to think so.

Although my dad did not officially belong to this church, he attended almost all of the services and for a while was a member of the choir. I can remember turning around, looking up and seeing him holding the hymnal and singing joyfully Sunday after Sunday.

In addition to the choir dad also took part in other activities including the annual Christmas Party. This was where the children of the parish were encouraged to bring in gifts for less fortunate children and where Santa Claus himself appeared to hand out presents to "all the good little boys and girls." I did not know for years that my dad was the Santa Claus. I only knew that when my time came I ran up to him, sat on his lap and had the usual conversation. "Have you been a good girl, what would you like for Christmas?"

The story goes that dad was able to pull this off for years until one year my brother climbed up on his lap and said, "Hi dad." It was at this point that dad turned this impersonation over to someone else.

One of the most important activities of the year was the annual

Christmas pageant. This was an opportunity for the children, dressed as nativity characters to bring the happy message of Christmas to the entire congregation. Of course each child was hoping for a special part and would eagerly await the passing out of the piece of paper indicating which role they would play. There were Shepards, the Wise Men, Angels, and the leading characters, Joseph, Mary and the baby Jesus. I of course always wanted to play the Virgin Mary, even from my earliest recollection I have as a young child who always it seemed played the role of a Shepard.

Year after year I would reach for the paper and there in printed word was the answer, "Shepard." As the years went by I would watch and listen and sort of "take notes" on the Virgin Mary. I watched how she walked, listened intently to what she said and how she said it and to me the most important of all, how she looked. Over and over again I dreamed that one day this role would be mine. For now the lovely blonde seemed to get it and I could only wait.

One year a surprise happened. I could see it in the face of the teacher. There would be a change. The papers were handed out and I eagerly reached for mine. A new word appeared on the paper, "Wiseman." Wiseman, I could only question this. I was a girl, how could I play the role of a Wiseman? How could I not be chosen for the leading role of Mary? Why, I was growing up, or so I thought and for sure was old enough to assume this awesome responsibility. Once again I slouched down in my seat and waited and sure enough, the lovely blond got the role of Mary. Talking to God seemed to make no difference. Was there no justice? Wiseman indeed!

When the time came to walk down the aisle there I was in brown-stripped cloth, paper crown on my head and in my hands the token to be presented to the Christ Child. Looking up I could hardly contain my sadness although I had to admit "she" did look nice. Just what was her secret?

As the years went by I continued to play the roles assigned to me including the time I did get to play the "important" angel standing behind the tiny family.

And then it happened! In a year that I thought was to be like the others, I reached for my paper wondering if it would be Shepard, Wiseman or Angel? Imagine my surprise when the word, "Virgin Mary" appeared. For a moment I just sat there stunned. Did the teacher mean this, was there a mistake, did she hand me the wrong piece of paper, what should I do? I looked up and staring back at me with a broad grin on her face the teacher indicated that indeed there had been no mistake; I was to play the role of the Virgin Mary! Just the thought of it sent shivers up and down my spine. I could hardly contain my excitement, I WAS the Virgin Mary!

Each day in my attic room I practiced saying the few words attributed to Mary and walked as I thought Mary would have done. This was my chance and I was not going to blow it. I was the Virgin Mary and everyone in the congregation would see that I was the best one so far. As the day approached I wondered how I would look in the flowing blue robe and the white shawl on my head? And to top it off I was to wear sandals on my feet and not the brown tie shoes that I wore in other pageants. I could hardly wait for the night of the Christmas Pageant!

Throughout all of the preparations I tried very hard to keep in mind that this was a religious event and not a contest but for this little girl the idea of walking down the aisle in a blue robe was the ultimate! At last I was good enough to be Mary.

When the evening finally arrived I could hardly wait to get to the church. There I found the ironed costume carefully laid out along with bobby pins to hold the shawl to my head and the sandals someone had lent for the occasion. As I dressed I thought about the long walk down the aisle. I had been carefully instructed on just how to do it. "Walk slowly and carefully, lean a little on Joseph as if it is difficult for you to walk." After all, this was the time when they were heading to the stable for the night.

The music began and we were off. Joseph played a good part and did exactly what he was supposed to do. He took my arm and showed his concern. I on the other hand, trying as best as I could to remember the instructions and the solemnity of the occasion, sort of swaggered down the aisle. I tried not to make it look that way and did just enough leaning and looking at Joseph to make it have the right effect. But I could not help myself; the swagger just seemed to take over. I thought I hid it well and hopefully not too many parishioners noticed. But swagger I did.

The rest of the play went off as rehearsed. Everyone remembered their lines, the tiny babe in the manger did not cry until almost the end. After the performance the congregation gathered downstairs for the party and of course, the arrival of Santa. Nothing that year, not the cookies or the gift from Santa came anywhere near the role of the Virgin Mary.

I kept the outfit on until finally my Sunday School teacher gently reminded me that it was time to take it off. The Shepards and angels and even the Wise Men had removed their costumes right after the end of the pageant. But I was determined to hold on as long as I could.

Years later while rummaging through old photos I came across a picture from one of the pageant years. I can be seen on the left side of the picture kneeling between the other two Wise Men, the paper crown on my head and the baloney curls falling to my shoulders. In the center is the tiny family and the lovely blond Virgin Mary. I am not sure any pictures exist of me in my role as Mary but that's fine. I was the Virgin Mary, I played the role, I wore the robe and that's all that counts.

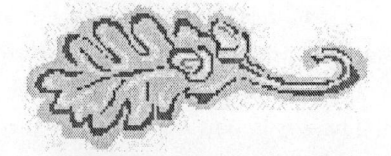

Discovering More Than Sand And Sun

Discovering More Than Sand and Sun

During many of my youthful years we had a delightful repose that took place in the month of August. It was much anticipated by young and old alike. We made preparations, packed our bags, loaded the car and set off on a Friday evening so as to be there when morning arrived. By the time dad dismounted from the South Leonard Street bus and hurriedly climbed the stairs, the house was full of packages, boxes, suitcases and assorted supplies that one might think a small army brigade was about to embark on a military mission. There was nothing left to chance. All bases were covered. You took everything you thought you might need and even things you didn't think you would need but took anyway just in case you changed your mind and ended up needing them.

The time of departure was rather late due to the amount of time spent on packing, preparing and the loading of the car. But off we did go eagerly anticipating a wonderful week in a heavenly place. We were off to Cape Cod, the mere mention of it sending ripples of joy throughout all of us. I believe I was almost nine years old before setting foot on this glorious place. My mom's brother had purchased a home and land in West Yarmouth and subsequently built a number of cottages, one of which we were to occupy for the week.

I don't remember the first trip but mom says it was extremely difficult. Grammy was still with us and we were bringing her to the Cape to see the family. Now in addition to all the necessary things needed for our little family of four, there were the things that only Grammy needed. These included the commode, special medicines, and various apparatus that only a young child might find complicated.

The story goes that as the last piece of "stuff" was placed in the car, Grammy had a "bad spell". I never quite knew just what that meant but it usually meant a delay in whatever was happening. My brother and I were told to remove ourselves from the action and to entertain ourselves until things calmed down. Good old Grammy, she always seemed to pull through and the adventure was again on schedule. It was not until I was much older that I really knew how very sick she was and how much time and effort it was for mom and dad to tend to her.

Most of the years the trip took place when all of the interstates had not been completed and so our sojourn took us through many a small town and large city. We had instructions from mom to keep quiet when dad came to an intersection and had to follow the very small signs leading us to the next part of the trip. For some reason when we approached Providence whoa to the kid who opened their mouth when dad was concentrating on his driving. Mom would turn herself around and give us "the look".

Finally the Cape Cod Canal came into view and the bridge to paradise was only a mile or so away. As I mentioned most of these trips took place in the night and so by the time we were crossing the bridge, we were all beginning to yawn and yawn some more. But for those who have a love affair with Cape Cod you know exactly what I am talking about.

Once on the Cape we journeyed some miles to reach our destination. By now it was really late and we were not supposed to make any noise so as not to wake anyone up. We would remain in the car, heads drooped onto someone or something, and there remain until we heard folks stirring in the main house. Once we did we tumbled out of the car and there was hugging and kissing for everyone. The family included my uncle, my aunt and two cousins, the girl older than my brother and the boy younger than me.

We could hardly wait to get the keys to the cottage and to unpack our things. What joy awaited us! As soon as the unpacking was completed we were off to the beach to "check it out," the waves always tempting us to don our suits and jump in. Then it was off to the grocery store to get the items that we needed (just in case we needed something we forgot to pack or deliberately thought we would not need).

The week seemed to fly past. We swam, walked the streets of the tiny villages, looked in store windows at things that could be found in elegant shops on the Cape and in places like Miami and Palm Beach. For these occasions dad would wear his Bermuda shorts and mom and I would wear our sun dresses. I would save my money throughout the year and use it to buy fancy socks or some piece of clothing for the coming school year. Our shopping was mostly window shopping but somehow we never felt sad that we couldn't buy things, we were too busy having fun in paradise.

Even meals were different. I had raisin bran in the morning, a treat from the standard corn flakes or oatmeal. Sometimes dad and I would go to a bakery and get cranberry muffins hot out of the oven. Lunch was mostly at the beach, sandwiches with a compliment of fruit, lemonade and cookies.

Not only did we have fun during this week but there was always surprises, some good and some we would rather not have experienced. On one occasion mom almost lost her new dentures in the surf. She did not think it funny at all but dad and us kids howled with laughter. Then there was the hurricane when dad took me to see the pounding surf and the downed trees and power lines. He took pictures and I stood next to him hoping for more action.

One year was significantly very important for me. I was just about thirteen and entering the time in a young ladies life that held changes to mind, body and soul. I had been swimming with my cousin and we were in her bedroom changing from bathing suits into dry shorts and tee shirts. Another girl of about my age was there changing as well. As we all disrobed from our wet, uncomfortable suits I could not help but notice that both of them had breasts that were significantly larger than mine.

Up to now I was not too worried. I figured it was going to happen soon and finally I would be among the young ladies who now wore a bra. I could hardly wait. But as I glanced at my two companions I became somewhat disturbed. Perhaps, I thought, I am delayed, perhaps there is something wrong and I won't grow breasts at all. All kinds of scenarios raced through my mind as I turned my back so they wouldn't see me.

I quickly undressed and put on dry clothes praying no one would even look at me. That night before bed I decided to see if I might hurry things along. There had to be something I could do, some vitamin to take, some action to perform. I decided to pull and stretch myself as much as possible. Perhaps if I could just move things along, perhaps a little tugging would help. And so I began this daily regiment, this ritual hoping that my breasts would finally begin to grow.

Looking back at the absurdity of my actions and the irrational thinking that accompanied those actions I can only laugh. "All things in due time," I believe the saying goes. But for someone who grew up in time when such things were not discussed at least not in our house, this was a time of concern and anxiety. I wanted to be like my cousin with a bathing suit packed at the top with just the right amount of natural filling. After all high school was just around the corner and I desperately wanted to be just like other girls.

As summer faded and the annual seasonal change occurred , a change began to take place in my body as well. Can you imagine? I was finally getting breasts. This delightful occurrence allowed me the delicious thought that very soon I could wear a bra and next summer I would change from my wet bathing suit into dry clothes and not turn around at all.

Pink Satin

Pink Satin

This week I had the pleasure of once again shopping for bras. I say pleasure in jest of course. For me shopping for bras has not been a delight since I was thirteen and accompanied my mother to Brown Brothers Department Store on North Main Street. Oh, the excitement of it all!

At last I was going to be just like the other girls in class who wore the latest fashion in bras. Finally I was joining all the girls in the "sorority of the bra wearers." What a day for me. I could hardly wait to get to the store. To this day I can still remember it in vivid detail. Looking back, I am amazed that such a commonplace activity could be so monumental in my life and the subject of a story. But it was just that. A significant occasion, one to be remembered long after the bra wore out and was discarded. It was a beginning of a new chapter in my life.

Brown Brothers store was a typical "dry goods" store of the day. It was where you went for everything from top to bottom, including shoes and of course bras. Because of the shoe trade it always smelled of new leather. Articles of clothing lay in piles on old-fashioned display tables separated by department including clothing for young ladies. Since we had been going to Brown Brothers for years mom knew the sales people quite well. We were always greeted by name with a polite good morning or good afternoon. On this day mom chose one of the ladies to help us with this significant purchase.

According to my timetable it seemed like it had taken me a forever to develop than just about everyone else in class. At times I was convinced that I would never have breasts no matter how I tugged and pulled I remained flat as could be.

In gym class or on the way home from school the girls would

talk about wearing bras. I was mortified. I was still wearing cotton undershirts and knew without a doubt that you could see them through my blouses. What distress it caused me. Mom did her best to alleviate my fears and explain how things happen but of course the explaining that one got back in those days paled in comparison to all of the books, classes, and TV discussions about growing up that children get today.

For years I was sure that the chest area of my body was just not doing what is was supposed to do. I was flat, no bones about it. Try as I may to push and pull on that part of my anatomy I remained flat, flat as could be. The horror of it all! I remember a summer when I was at my cousin's house on Cape Cod and her and another girl were changing to go swimming. How could I take off my blouse I thought? God, what would they think?

One day however, when mom sensed my distress, she took me by the hand and we climbed the attic stairs. I could not imagine how going to the attic could make me feel better but I went anyway. She rummaged around for a while looking for a particular box. When she found it she called to me to come and sit beside her.

She opened the box and gently lifted the articles from within. There were odd pieces of lace, tiny pin cushions decorated with make believe strawberries, a couple of ladies slips and blouses and there on the bottom of the box was a lovely pink satin bra. Mom held it up for me to see. As with everything else this too had a story. Mom could tell me exactly when and where this bra came from. This had been her first "real" bra.

I couldn't wait to try it on. Would it fit? Could you see it through my blouses? At last it would replace my old fashioned under shirts.

Mom helped me into it and then right there in the attic it happened. I was at last grown up. I couldn't wait to wear it to school. Never mind that is was not new like the other girls. Never mind that it had funny straps that wound around you and hooked in the front. Never mind that it did not have rows and rows of stitching that made the cups stick out like a child's party hat. Nothing mattered. The only thing that mattered was that I at last was just like every girl in class. I now wore a bra.

The Rose Of Sharon

The Rose Of Sharon

I don't recall when I was growing up that my mom spent a whole lot of time in the garden. She does love plants and gently tends beautiful violets and other houseplants however, actually seeing her digging in the dirt, planting or weeding does not come to mind. I'm sure she would have liked to garden, but necessity dictated that her time and energy be spent in other ways. There were children who needed tending and an elderly, bedridden mother to care for.

In the years before my remembering, she did garden and reports she enjoyed it immensely. I recall stories of the gardens in the city and the garden at the lake. In fact, the story goes that mom was gardening when my arrival became evident and she took time to wash her feet well so she would be presentable to the hospital staff.

Our Victorian home had several gardens, quite large ones on either side of the huge grape arbor in the back and long narrow ones that ran the length of the house on the driveway side. These gardens contained plants and flowers that had been planted years before by my grandparents and by the Italian family who rented the downstairs apartment. There were old-fashioned climbing roses, perennials of every size and sort, small trees and an odd assortment of plants from a myriad of Easters that always ended up in the garden. There was even evidence of tomato stakes and vegetable patches. Hollyhocks, both pink and white, greeted us as we went up and down the driveway.

Around the backyard gardens were fences that time and use had twisted and turned into several shapes. There were some that you could actually hang on to and ride and others that were short and intended to just define the garden space. Amazingly, these fences never quite needed mending and when we moved from there they were at least 60 years old.

In the front of the house was mom's pride and joy. The Rose of Sharon tree held a position of importance, not only because it was seen from the street, but because in Mom's heart it stood for memories of long ago. This bent and twisted tree was pushed in growth so that it stood out in front and was flat on the porch side of the house. Each year glorious buds and blossoms would greet us and mom would again relate the story of "the tree planting." The tree covered the view from the front porch on the first floor and was tall enough to present its branches and flowers to those who gazed out of the second floor windows.

Mom would take the time to check the branches to make sure there were no breaks or any branches that were drooping. If she found one, she would gather string or twine and tie it up to prevent further damage, often calling upon anyone walking by on the sidewalk to stop and help her hold the branch while she tied. There was only the smallest patch of dirt that held this tree, then our fence and finally, on the other side of the fence, the sidewalk where the tree hung down for passerbys to dodge on their walk. The amazing thing is that I do not recall anyone reaching up to pull on the tree or to break a branch that was in the way. It was the unwritten rule that this tree was off limits to such endeavors.

As children we were instructed that the tree was off limits for climbing. It was far too delicate and mom was very protective. All tree climbing took place in the backyard where you were free to climb and explore and imagine to your heart's content. This tree was special, to be admired and cared for as a family heirloom.

Family albums contain numerous pictures taken in front of the tree. The oldest photo's showing grandma and grandpa and various relatives and friends from a time past. There they stand, long flowing dresses, huge flowered hats and men in quite dignified britches and coats. I try to make out faces but since I was not around I must rely on mom's still keen memory and these worn, tattered photo's. It was evident though that even then the tree held a position of importance. "Here's Aunt Nellie and oh yes, there's Uncle Joe," she would say. "That's when they came to show off "their Ethel." Look, this picture is when my dad came home from his first day of work, how proud he was." And so the stories were told and so I learned about these lives and people and joys and sorrows. Back then the tree looked so much younger and smaller, and the yard mostly dirt like the street and sidewalk.

As the years wore on and our departure from our home became evident, mom sensed that the tree must remain. She would go and tend to it even as the construction crews began to demolish neighboring homes. She pruned the branches, tied up the drooping ones and watered it with the hose when the ground became dry and parched.

Soon heavy construction vehicles became a common site in the neighborhood. They wound their way up and down the street carrying their loads of equipment one way and on the return trip, loaded with the vestiges of what had been a neighborhood home. These vehicles stirred up clouds of dust and dirt as they traveled by the house increasingly the deposits would cover our clapboards, shutters, and of course the Rose of Sharon tree. When this happened, Mom would stop what she was doing, and lovingly water the tree to remove the dust and ensure the flowers continued to "decorate" our lives.

Little by little we packed away boxes containing every imaginable family treasure. There was cut glass, family pictures, trinkets of jewelry, old gold frames containing pictures of grandma and grandpa, assorted aunts, uncles, cousins and faces that smiled in front of the tree. It was a difficult time for mom. She was leaving the family homestead and all of the memories of her life. The impending demolition was to make way for a new highway, and she, the caretaker of family heirlooms felt an obligation to ensure that she take as much as possible. It was understood that we, my brother and I were to know and remember and of course, carry on our lives with what she could bring with her.

On the day of our final departure from South Leonard Street, mom stood in front of the tree, gently stroking its branches and gazing at the pink buds and flowers. Dad asked if she wanted to break some branches to take with us, but she declined. This tree was to remain as she remembered, complete and beautiful, a representative of a family today and a time from long ago.

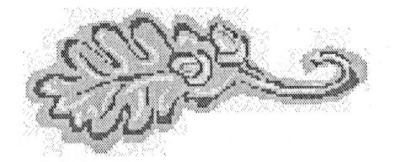

I Was A Privileged Child

I Was a Privileged Child

In many ways I was a privileged child. Not that I grew up in a mansion or went to private schools or even had a coming out gala. There were no trips to Europe, no chauffeurs, no domestic help or nannies. I didn't shop on Fifth Avenue, I didn't go to a private girl's camp off in another state. We were never written up in the society column and I cannot trace my ancestors to anyone other than plain working class people. For most of my growing years I lived in a very old Victorian house on a busy city street. The front windows looked out upon railroad tracks and a huge lumber company surrounded by a fence. The city bus ran in front of our house and the smoke from the trains turned everything on the front porch black.

But believe it or not I was privileged. Privilege as defined in Webster's Dictionary means "a right or immunity granted as a peculiar benefit, advantage, or favor." Did I have an advantage, was I granted a peculiar benefit? I think so. It was only with age that I realized it. Let me explain.

My life, although somewhat chaotic at times was a reasonably happy childhood. I was born to parents who truly loved each other and showed it throughout their lives. We did not have much money and learning to "make do" was taught at an early age. After some years we not only owned the house (having inherited it from Grandma) but in addition we had a summer home. It was not quite ours, but owned by my paternal grandmother. It was a perfect place to enjoy the carefree moments of childhood. For me that was quite the thing since most of the neighbors and friends just lived in one home, usually a city dwelling like ours.

The very beginning years of my childhood I can only relate to by stories told by my parents, some black and white photographs and a few brief, if I try hard enough, personal recollections. As I became older (grammar school age) I developed an uncanny ability to recall the intimate details of people and places that played a role in my life. I call it a kind of memory trap. For instance, I can remember my great uncle's home in the northeast corner of the state and the long trips to get there. I remember the smell was so different from our city home. His home was in the country with cow pastures all around and he lived there along with my grandmother and great grandfather. When great uncle and great grandfather died the house was sold and Grammy moved to the lake property.

As with most other things in our lives everything was a production. The ride took hours and hours and the car was always full to the brim with stuff. I remember getting car sick and riding through all the tiny towns along the way. Uncle's house was set back from the road and had a large barn/garage and chicken coops in the rear. It bordered a very large dairy farm which became an exciting place to revel in country life. It was here I fed the cows in the stalls that were waiting to be milked, drank the warm milk mixed with Hershey's Syrup, fished in the little river that crisscrossed the farm, and watched intently the farm chores being done. And believe it or not, I rode the little wagon suspended on a pulley that carried the manure to the end of the barn where it was dumped onto a pile.

Ah the smell of the great outdoors, manure, chicken yards and more. To this day the odor you get if by some chance you are lucky enough to drive by a farm is more welcoming to me that obnoxious. A heady reminder of that long ago farm.

Privilege meant a weekly ride in the old Chevy or Dodge and perhaps an ice cream cone along the way. It meant having one of the largest Christmas trees in the neighborhood, holiday dinners eating off good dishes that had been handed down from generation to generation, listening to a record player and of course the attic filled to the brim with treasures.

Growing up we never had an automatic washing machine or dryer. But mom took pains to starch and iron my clothes so that I would always look like a young lady. When Grammy died mom removed the pretty colored ribbons from the flower arrangements and ironed them carefully. She then made me a white dress with tabs around the waist where the ribbons were threaded. It brought many a compliment that summer.

Privilege meant that Christmas morning was glorious. Although there were few presents, the ones we received were magic. There was the beautiful baby doll almost the size a real baby that was dressed in the most beautiful pink outfit. One year when I was older I received a package with black velvet material and a pattern for a new dress. It was spectacular. Another year dad received a bird bath and he and my brother spent the day floating toy boats and making up stories.

Privilege meant being able to go to the Girl's Club on the bus all by myself. Here I learned how to make an apron and cook things like tuna casserole and sugar cookies. Why I even enrolled in a *Charm Class* but that is another story.

Mom and dad felt that children were to be taken along with them whenever possible. It was their feeling that we were to be exposed to all kinds of situations and to use different experiences as background for our development. Therefore I got to go to all sorts of things like meetings, conventions, and even funerals. I learned at an early age the appropriateness of wearing hats and gloves and easily conversing with an assortment of adults. Today collecting ladies gloves is very popular and of course, what else, I have just such a collection.

Privilege also meant there were things we did not have. Again this was due to financial concerns and also the feeling that one must work and earn for themselves. We never felt deprived or sorry for ourselves. We explored our world through books, trips to the library, rides in the old Chevy through back roads and city streets. I was surrounded with reminders of family through old picture albums and cartons of antiques.

I had a new white dress for grammar school graduation, a charcoal wool jumper from the Lord and Taylor bargain bin for the first day of high school and money for the bus. When the time came I even attended college, the first in my family to do so.

Why of course I was a privileged child of that I have no doubt although it took me until adulthood to realize it. I just figured that everyone lived as we did. I knew from rides and vacations that other people had finer homes, elegant clothes and expensive cars. On rare occasions we dined in lovely restaurants usually to celebrate someone's birthday. I know mom always found a way to come up with a few extra dollars.

One summer we even went all the way to Niagara Falls! Grammy had died the previous November and I think dad thought it would be good for mom. We again rode through little towns and villages finally arriving at the falls. As we approached we could hear the mighty thunder of the falls and could hardly wait to set eyes on it. We stayed in cottages not far from the tourist section and spent days just looking at the splendor and the magnificence of the area.

I took my doll with all the newly starched doll clothes packed in a small metal trunk that had been mom's, the one in which she too had packed her doll clothes when she accompanied her parents on various adventures.

While on the trip we had a chance to go on the Maid of the Mist boat, a tourist attraction that took riders very close to the falls. It was not until many years later that I learned just why mom chose to stay behind on the dock as dad and us kids enjoyed the thrilling adventure. There was only so much money and it had to be used sparingly in order to make the trip last a few more days.

Did we have fun, did we come away with wonderful memories, were we excited? You bet! I am delighted that I can now "spoil" my children with only the best life has to offer. What more could a parent ask for?

The Camping Trip

The Camping Trip

Years ago when we had very little money, many young children and only a week for vacation we set out in our trusty Volkswagen bus for a trip to a shoreline camp ground in a neighboring state. I had seen an article in a magazine listing all of the attractions and charming places that you could visit. It sounded like a nice place to go so I contacted the camp ground and made reservations. We could hardly wait for the adventure to begin.

The week before I spent packing clothes, shoes, linens, sleeping bags, toys for the beach and the campground, medical supplies, tools and an assortment of any and all things that just might come in handy during the week. In addition there was the tent, cots, stools, table, camp stove, lanterns, flash lights, cooking utensils, cooler and boxes of food. With little money in our pockets I knew that I had to have enough meals and snacks for the week. Baking and preparing meals took up much of the week.

Getting ready was no small feat. We had purchased a small, home-made wooden tag-a-long trailer that looked very similar to a dog house on wheels. It took a bit of doing to stand up on a chair, bend over the top (where it opened) and place the articles into the trailer in such a way as to have the necessary ones on top, you know things like toilet paper and diapers. I worked from a list but was sure that something would be missing when we arrived at our camp site.

On the day of our departure, with all the paraphernalia stored on board and the children in their assigned seats we headed off for the (what we thought would be a) six hour trip. The skies looked a bit menacing but we were convinced that we could outrun the storm and arrive at our destination without much concern. I was wrong. About half way into the trip while we were on the turnpike the heavens opened up and the rain began to fall. It was one of those rain storms when you could hardly see a few feet in front of you. The bus began to hydroplane, the rain came in torrents and the hair pulling and feet touching began. I was determined to keep the peace and to try to keep the four children from killing each other while my husband concentrated on the driving.

By now we had run out of songs to sing, automobile games to play, and everyone was getting on everyone else's nerves. "How much longer? I'm hungry. I have to pee. I think I am going to throw up." It was no small feat to keep one's sanity for the duration of the trip. Finally we reached the campground and registered. John ran from the bus to the office and came out a few minutes later looking a bit bedraggled but with a look that said, "At last we've arrived."

It was now time to find the camp site, set up the tent, bring in the supplies and gear, cook the supper and bed the children down for the night. I began to talk to myself, "OK don't loose it now. Just because it is still raining we can do this with a little ingenuity." John was talking to himself too but his words (the ones I could make out) were a little more colorful.

Arriving at our site it was quickly evident that this task was going to be no small feat. The first order of business was to set up the tent which John immediately proceeded to do. "Can I help daddy? I want to get out. I'm hungry." And the big one, "I have to pee." Calmly I told the children that we had to be quiet and wait for a few minutes while daddy set up the tent. Four little faces with noses pressed to the steamy glass watched intently as daddy tried his best to accomplish this impressive task. I could make out some of the words he spoke and did my best to ensure the children could not make them out.

Finally and with much valor John had the tent up. One by one he carried the children to the tent with implicit instructions not to touch the tent in any way. For those die hard campers you know that if you run your finger along the tent roof the path is open for rain to come in. Once the children were in the tent we began the trek from van to tent to bring in supplies running in between the downpour that was still intense. It was not but a few moments when we heard the words, "She's touching the tent." And then the dreaded, "The rain is coming in!"

I decided that I would calmly instruct her (and the boys just in case they decided to do the same) about why we do not touch the top of the tent when it is raining. As I turned to leave, I heard the words, "She's doing it again." Now, as I turned around slowly I thought this is enough. Forget the words, now it's time for action! "OK" I said. "One more time young lady and you are in trouble, do you hear me?" Hoping against all odds and knowing my darling daughter as I did I had a funny feeling that she was not through.

By this time water was leaking into the tent around the sides of the floor. Poor hubby, the sport, grabbed a shovel, rolled up his trousers, removed his shoes and proceeded to trench around the tent hoping this would take care of that problem. I dug into the food boxes and came up with the peanut butter, jelly, and a knife and proceeded to feed the now agitated mob. My directive was to enjoy the sandwich and not to ask for anything more. Right about this time I began to notice again an uncomfortable feeling that had started in the morning before we even got onto the road and thought to myself, not this, not now. Just when my body was answering me with an answer I would have preferred to neglect, I heard THOSE words again, "She's doing it again!"

This time with the coolness of a marine drill sergeant who is tired, hungry and frustrated at the lack of cooperation by his recruits I headed for the corner in which SHE sat. "That's it young lady. No more talking." I then took measures to ensure she would not be able to reach the top of the tent. All eyes were on me. Needless to say there was not a word spoken and in spite of the torrential downpour, total silence crept into the tent. I began to realize that no one had even asked to use the toilet in the last hour. That was about to change.

In the middle of this madness a voice cried out, "I have to pee right now!" I reached for my raincoat and bundled up the third child as best as I could and proceeded to head for the bathrooms. By this time the anticipated joy of a week of fun was rapidly loosing out to a more gloomy outlook. "Just who's idea was this anyway?"

I answered my own question and decided not to bring up the subject to my "trenching" husband.

When I approached the bathrooms I could make out some muttering voices and a line of folks who definitely did not look happy. Approaching, I asked, "What happened, can we use the bathroom?" With a curt answer a woman replied, "Let's put it this way, if you live anywhere close by I would suggest you pack up and go home." I thought to myself, "Why lady, home is almost 6 hours away (on a good day) and we've come for a week of fun and relaxation. I'm not going to let a little rain spoil our camping trip." Ha!

Because God in his wisdom had made it easier for a male child, we took advantage of a group of small trees and bushes and the deed was accomplished. Now if only SHE would forget to heed the call we might be able to bed down and wake to a sparkling sunlit morning. Oh the joy of anticipation!

Due to the storm the evening was darker earlier therefore bedtime came a little earlier than usual. It was lights out (flashlights) and we finally crept into our sleeping bags. It was not too long when we heard the sounds of a crash. One of the double decker cots had fallen over and the oldest child lay on the damp floor. "Are you hurt?" I asked. "No but my pajamas are all wet." Sliding out from my bag I scrambled to find a dry pair for him. The only one's I could come up with were his sister's, pink poodles galore! "Mom I can't wear these they are HERS." "Look just put them on for tonight and we will find yours in the morning." "NO!" "OK I said, go to bed naked." The poor child just stood there looking at me as though I had completely lost my mind. It took a few minutes but find his I did. Reaching over I gave him a big hug and a kiss, told him I loved him and helped him back into the now damp sleeping bag.

His brother who had been on the top bunk was luckier. He happened to fall and land right on the duffle bags that had been put up on plastic sheeting. So far he was fine just stunned as he woke up as he was moving through the air. He too got a hug and a kiss and a hand as he struggled to climb up to the top bunk again. My husband was in a deep sleep and did not even hear the commotion.

Somewhere in the wee hours of the morning I finally did fall asleep. While trying to "catch it" as dad would say, I tried to put happy thoughts in my mind and say a few prayers for a sunny day tomorrow. Morning, how did I know? The little voices woke me with their conversation that went something like this, "Ha ha you fell out of bed last night. So what you got wetter" . . . The littlest one just smiled and waited for a diaper change. "Thank you God."

After breakfast (bought donuts and juice) it was time to hang out the sleeping bags to dry and time to set up camp in the normal way a serious, often time camper would do. The children busied themselves with the toys we brought and I began to think that perhaps this week would not be so bad after all. Little did I know. Because we had planned on spending time at the beach and hurray, today was the first day, with excitement we loaded the VW with beach toys, towels, blankets, sun tan lotion, food and folding chairs, umbrellas and we were off.

Arriving at the beach we soon found another catastrophe—there were incredibly high tides (the torrential rains were part of the front) and a jeep with sirens whirling by at unannounced times as the crew sped to rescue swimmers from dangerous tides. In addition to this bedlam the evening hours were spent in the VW bus watching as a truck carrying a huge sprayer drove through each camping area to spray for mosquitoes.

My condition worsened, the littlest one got a diaper rash, the rains continued, the spraying continued, the clothes, towels and sleeping bag liners smelled horribly and all of us began to make noises about going home. And so, at (not quite) the end of the week we packed it all in again and headed home. Thinking that this had to be the most horrible vacation we ever had I over heard the children laughing and talking, "Remember when you fell out of bed, remember when mom tied you up, remember how mom took the hotdogs into the bus as the big spray truck came by . . ." This was followed by laughter and delight.

That night as we put the children to bed we heard the words, "Can we do that again?"

Uncle Vic

Uncle Vic

When my mother-in-law passed away we inherited the usual family objects and memorabilia that had been hers throughout her life. These remembrances consisted of a few sets of dishes, some jewelry, photo albums and a few trinkets and decorations from her home. In addition we also inherited her plate collection which had been lovingly displayed on specially constructed shelves in her kitchen. These plates were her pride and joy and she would talk about them to whomever came into the house. "Look, here is the plate my cousin brought from Canada and the one from Florida, and over here is the plate from our fortieth wedding anniversary." Each year more plates were added to the collection by friends and family who knew how much she enjoyed receiving them.

Toward the end of her life she would tell me that these plates were to be mine and then they were to be passed down to our children. Today, twenty three years after her death they remain in dusty cartons in our basement not having seen the light of day since her death. Last summer while rummaging in the dirt basement of their trailer in New Hampshire our youngest son discovered four plates of Grams. I think she may have brought these four as reminders of the collection in her home in Connecticut. We decided to leave them in New Hampshire.

In addition to the material inheritances and unlike inheritances of other people, we also inherited a person, someone we called Uncle Vic. Uncle Vic was Grandma's brother, a quiet, gentle man whose life was something of a mystery. He stood almost six feet tall and his body was very lean, a sort of "Jack Sprat." In the early years of our marriage folks hardly spoke of him except for the occasional mention of his name.

Uncle Vic lived the life of a recluse in the woods of Northern Maine very close to the Canadian border. We were told that he was a man who was more comfortable living in his small house heated only by wood than he was anywhere else. One summer while vacationing in that part of Maine my in-laws took movies of the beauty found in the region of the Allagash. These eight mm movies also included footage of Uncle Vic and his humble surroundings. A quick nod of the head and a simple wave were all we saw of him.

Years later his other sister insisted that he be brought to our state and there to reside (comfortably) for his last years. Uncle Vic never said much about the move but we all assumed he would have preferred to remain in his beloved woods deep in the heart of Maine.

When he arrived he was set up in an apartment in the city, a kind of old folks brick structure close to the center of town. He did not come with much, just a few articles of clothing, his army discharge papers, and a few personal items. At the end of his life and after living in the city for many years he still had only a few belongings, a few articles of clothing, a few personal items and his army discharge papers. In his wallet we found an old tattered photo of Uncle Vic as a young man standing next to an attractive young woman in a stylist fur coat. They had their arms around each other and as you looked at the picture you almost knew that they might have been in love.

Uncle Vic was always included in our family gatherings. He would put on his one dress shirt and pants and usually a sleeveless sweater and wait for one of us to pick him up. Although he was a man of few words, he seemed to enjoy himself in the company of the family. He would sit quietly and speak hesitantly only if spoken to. His command of the English language both written and spoken was not good and we did not speak French. The children drew pictures and made little gifts for him just as they did for their grandparents and he seemed to appreciate their little gestures of love. At Christmas we would buy presents and label them as coming from him. He again seemed to enjoy the festivities and the handing out of gifts to the family.

When my mother-in-law passed away John and I took over the care of Uncle Vic. He did not require much at first, only the weekly visit to his apartment to make sure he was OK and to bring the few groceries he requested. In addition, we accompanied him to his doctor's appointments. As time went on his care became more intense. He was failing in health and we would receive a call from the apartment staff indicating that Uncle Vic was not well. On those occasions we would go to him and oftentimes take him to the hospital via an Emergency Room visit.

I thought it kinda funny that he always wore his long johns even in the summer. On one of the frequent trips to the ER the doctor asked him some questions to determine his mental state. One of those questions was, "Do you know who the president of the United States is?" Uncle Vic pondered for a moment and then replied, "Yes, Harry Truman." The year was 1982. The physician smiled at us and at Uncle Vic and said, "There's nothing wrong with this man, Truman was the last good president we had."

And so it went. The trips to the ER became more recurrent, the time spent with family became less frequent. In the end Uncle Vic was placed into a nursing home at the end of our street. He remained there for a very short time and then was gone. We received the call while we were in New Hampshire. On the ride home I had a few hours to think about his life and to plan for his funeral.

On the day of his funeral a small family gathered at the funeral home. There were no calling hours and only one spray of flowers next to his coffin. We stood talking about him and his life with us. We remarked at how good he looked in his new suit. Then we said our good byes and left for the church. Mom and I ended up helping to push him into the church on a gurney as there were not even enough men for pall bearers.

Uncle Vic is buried not far from our home in the same cemetery as his sisters. His wallet with the picture of the lady and his discharge papers have been placed in a box. I've never known anyone with so few belongings or so simple a life.

I hope in the end he was happy to have spent time with us, I wonder about the lady in the picture, would she have come to the funeral if she had known Uncle Vic had died?

The Pink Suit

The Pink Suit

In our family hand me downs were the norm. We didn't think of them quite like hand me downs, others castoffs, but rather the arrival of a box of treasures. As a child I received hand me downs from an assortment of friends and relatives, my cousin Ann for one and there were others. Through the years the memories of the exact items have faded but the knowledge that I did wear them remains.

Once in a while mom will remind me of an article of clothing and will tell me the story of how it came to be mine. Funny, but I can't remember where the clothes went when they became hand me downs to someone else. Even as I outgrew the child hand me downs I still seemed to acquire them; this time of course they were from adult to adult. One particular hand me down is a treasured memory.

Aunt Sara was the spinster aunt of my sister-in-law. She was a tiny slightly built lady with impeccable taste and a pocket book to match. Aunt Sara took pride in her appearance and it became evident to me from our first introduction that this lady enjoyed the amenities that money could provide. Oftentimes Aunt Sara would be a guest in our home joining family celebrations and would appear wearing the loveliest of attire.

During those years my clothes reflected mostly those of a stay at home mom. Certainly I had what would be referred to as "dress outfits", church, social engagements and so forth. I did my share of sewing and must admit usually looked quite nice. However, I was also to experience the "Sara years" in another way when for a short time I would acquire by way of hand me downs some of the most expensive outfits I would ever own and would appear at social engagements in this fine apparel.

One outfit that was most memorable was the "pink suit." Aunt Sara arrived at our house for one of these family occasions in a pink velvet suit. As pink was a favorite color of mine and velvet a favorite fabric I was particularly impressed. During the next few years the suit and Sara would make their appearance and I would imagine myself wearing the suit. It was above all my favorite item of dress. I could just hear the compliments now as I entered a room. My sister-in-law would wink at me and the understood message was clearly, "just hang in there and the suit will one day be yours."

As time passed and changes took place the hand me downs from Sara became fewer. Aunt Sara took ill and it was not long before she passed away. It was a sad time for my sister-in-law and family and I grieved also for this tiny wisp of a woman who was so generous.

On the evening of the wake I entered the funeral home on the arm of my husband. All around us were my sister-in-law's family members and friends waiting in line to view her body and pay respects. The line moved slowly as people knelt, prayed and then approached my sister-in-law to extend sympathy and spend a few moments talking with her. Soon I found myself approaching the coffin. This lady was not my relative nor was she particularly close to me, however, there was affection between us and her generosity had always impressed me, therefore before I knew it the tears began to flow.

As I waited in line I would occasionally hear someone comment on how nice Aunt Sara looked. Now it was my turn. I approached, knelt down and closed my eyes to say a prayer. When I opened them and looked at Aunt Sara there she was all decked out in the pink suit. For one split second I caught my breath and felt a smile break across my face. "Beautiful I thought, beautiful color, beautiful fabric, nice style. Good for you Sara, you go out in style."

At that moment my sister-in-law moved toward me and I moved toward her. With outstretched arms we embraced. "I'm so sorry," I said, "I know you will miss her." Just as I was saying my "sorry 's" my sister-in-law repeated the same words. "I'm so sorry," With a puzzled look on my face I noticed a slight smile cross hers. And at that moment we understood and laughed.

Aunt Sara went out in style alright, looking as she always did; elegant, chic, and just plain lovely and I, I had the memory of a lovely pint suit.

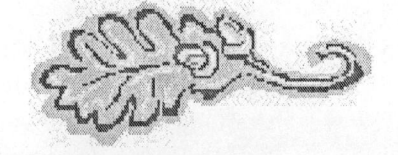

The White House

The White House

I grew up in a gray clapboard house many, many years ago. As I told you the house sat very close to the street, a busy street named South Leonard Street. That house, so different in size and character from my present residence was the house of my growing years. It was the house of growing years for many generations both family and tenant. It was a house filled to the peak with everything old. Old furniture, old walls and windows, old belongings of those long past away. Even the key to enter the door was old long, long before I came to be there.

I don't recall many new things ever arriving in this house. Everything I knew was there long before me and used over and over again. The house itself told stories and if you listened carefully you could hear them. One after another, time and time again.

Today I live in a big white house at the end of a circle far away from the gray clapboard house on the busy street known as South Leonard Street. This house, my white house, I had dreamt of from the time I knew that one day I would be married and living in my own home. Let me explain.

While the old Victorian house was home, certainly to all the assorted relatives who lived there one generation after another and by the very fact that I too, was of these generations. But this house, this white house is ours, one that belongs only to us, John and I and the children we made. It is the house that I dreamed of and longed for and waited for. Not the "picket fence" exactly but darn close.

Mom and dad loved to travel the highways and byways of the state. Sunday (and in our house, Monday too) was a time to get in our old Chevy or the Nash Rambler and roam around always looking here and there at the beautiful homes along the shore, in the hills of Litchfield or in the villages that bordered the

Connecticut River. One after another they would appear and ever so often there it would be—my white colonial house. I pictured how it would be living there. How I would decorate it, how I would make it mine?

It took us (John and I) many years to get here. We lived in several homes in several states before I came upon this place. Funny but I knew instantly that this was my home too. It was to be the dream come true. By today's standards this is a pretty ordinary house, you see them all over in many towns around here. In fact, it is a style that is chosen over and over again. But for me it was a dream come true, a coming home to a place I had always dreamed of.

One very cold and bleak January night my youngest son Christopher and I were returning home from shopping. I had seen an ad in the paper for this new development and I was anxious to visit the site. And so we drove down the streets and lanes to Heritage Hills Estates. My, I thought, what an impressive name! As luck would have it the model home was still open and in we went. And right there in the cold, unfinished kitchen I knew immediately that this was my dream house. I quickly toured the rest of the house and told the agent that we would be in touch. I could not wait to share the news with John.

Arriving home I was a flurry of words and descriptions and convinced him to come with me to see for himself. We arrived late on that same cold, bleak January night and drove to the site of what would become our home. There before us was a gigantic pile of dirt and nothing more. Not a tree, nor a branch or any living thing was to be seen. Only this mammoth pile of dirt cold to the touch, not for one moment neither giving forth the slightest encouragement nor thought of what might be there when the house was finally built.

With a hug and a kiss, we decided to call the agent and put down a deposit. I had never before picked out new pieces and parts for a home. Tomorrow would be the day I started to put my dream together.

That was in January and by June we were ready to move in. We had come to the site each day during those months to see for ourselves how the building was progressing. We would arrive camera in hand to record (as we did the lives of our children) the life of this home as it was unfolding.

This home was to be our family place for years to come. As with all homes, it would see sorrow and tears, life and death and all of the changes that were to take place within a growing family. I often wondered what my in-laws would think of this house. Grandpa left for New Hampshire shortly after the death of his wife years ago and there he remained only to come on rare occasions.

This house would not see diaper pails, cribs, dolls, small bikes and matchbox cars. This house would not see evening feedings and first days of school. No, this house would be home to older children who were busily making plans for college and jobs. Real cars took the place of bikes in the driveway, giggly phone messages were replaced with calls for dates and grown up vacation plans and Christmas stockings were never quite full of the fun things of childhood.

We arrived en mass with 4 grown children in tow and believe it or not seven vehicles. What we must have looked like to the neighbors as we rolled into town! Our garage became the place to pull an engine, do an oil change or string kayaks from the ceiling. All of this grown up activity contributed to the every day happenings at 45 Heritage Drive.

John and I planted each and every tree, blade of grass, shrub and even carried stones from a quarry to make garden paths. We delighted in making this yard our very own. Somehow the years went by, children moved out and rooms became empty. Our lovely white house was quieter, and emptier.

We now reflect on this house. It is big, too big for us. It is expensive to heat. The lawn, even with a new riding lawnmower takes time to cut. The bushes are grown, the herb garden almost overgrown, the paint is beginning to peel. Perhaps, we think, perhaps it is time to sell it. I look up the number of a real estate agency; I pick up the phone to dial. I return it to the cradle. Tomorrow, perhaps tomorrow I will make the call.

The Dance

The Dance

The day began as so many others had; the feeling of urgency washing over me like a rushing wave that catches you unexpectedly and causes you to panic. Coming down the exit ramp I looked for a place to run to. Straight ahead was the Regional Center for retarded citizens. Jamming on the breaks, I made a u-turn and parked as close as possible. Entering, I asked where I might find the ladies room. "Down the hall on the right." "Thanks," I said and quickly headed in that direction.

I could hear the voice of someone else in the room and although she was talking, I could not make out the words; it sounded like a gentle little voice, a sort of cooing sound. As I stood at the sink she came toward me, hand outstretched and gently laid it on my shoulder. "Where were you? I have been worried about you," she said. The look in her eyes was one of familiarity as though she truly knew me. For a moment I must have look puzzled to her. "There was a party last week and you weren't there, I was worried about you." I reached out my hand to her and replied, "Thank you. I am fine. I'm sorry I missed the party."

She kept her hand on my shoulder as the conversation continued and once again she asked, "Where were you, I was worried." And once again I replied, "I'm sorry I missed the party. I will try to get there the next time."

It dawned on me as I was speaking to her that here was a gentle soul reaching out to me at a time when I was in a hurry and really did not have time to waste. But looking into her eyes and feeling her touch and sensing her need to identify with me stopped me in my tracks. It became evident to me that a few more minutes of my time would make all the difference for this lady.

And so I began asking her some questions. "Do you like parties?"

"Oh yes," she replied, a smile beginning to arc across her face. "I am happy to go to some parties. I have fun and people like me there." As she was speaking, she again put her hand out to touch me, this time on the arm.

"What do you do when you go to a party?" "I get dressed up in my red dress and my red shoes, I like red, do you?" "Yes I do love red, as a matter of fact I once had a red party dress and I loved wearing it." "Do you still have the red dress?" she asked. "You know what, I think I do. I think I kept it all these years because I liked it so much." "Come to the party and wear your red dress like me. You can be my friend and dance with me and I will get you soda and chips and stuff."

She began to move around the room in a dancing motion, obviously not gracefully nor with movements that one usually identifies with dance but clearly a dance she had done before. She reached out her hands entwining them in mine and moved me carefully along with her and we stepped to the music from tile to tile and sink to stall and suddenly I began to move with her taking my direction from her lead. And then as if that were not enough, she and I began to hum and sing words to this unheard music. I cannot recall that the words made sense or that I could even make out an intelligible word but somehow it did not make any difference.

My new friend and I were somewhere else wearing our red dresses and dancing to the music. We were happy and having a wonderful time and somehow the urgency to be somewhere else and someplace else did not matter.

I don't know how long we enjoyed this kind of reverie, but I know as I moved to "our music" and "our dance" the time did not matter. All that mattered was the moment.

In a short time, although I cannot really be sure of how long of a time, we both began to let go. Her words were coming less and her humming stopped. She gradually removed her hands from mine and stepped back to look at me. "Thank you my friend," she said, the pronunciation of the words so very different from mine. "Thank you for dancing with me. Do you want me to get you soda and chips now?"

"That's OK, I do not think so, I really must be going now."

"Thank you my friend, thank you for dancing with me. Can you come to the party next time?"

"I would love to go to the party with you but I don't think I can. But I know when you go to your next party you will have a good time. You are a wonderful dancer and know just how to make someone happy."

I moved away from her and headed to the door. As I was leaving she called out, "the next time I will get you soda and chips because you are my friend and you know how to make me happy too."

To My First Grandchild

To My First Grandchild

I Loved You In My Dreaming

You are my first. You are the dream of my later years, the joy that comes only when I have been in a place the same as this and yet this place and time are so different. You are the materialization of wonderment, the longing for youth and the answer to prayer. You represent an extension of our lives, formed from the life who bore you and the life I gave to the one who bore you.

I try to pen the words that one day I shall leave for you to read. The words that hopefully will help you to understand my love for you, my longing for your being. Dreams can be elusive and sometimes we do not remember them or at least not all of them. But the dream of you and your coming was easy to recall. It was a frequent dream, the kind we love to remember and hope to repeat time and again. The kind of dream that makes you want to fall asleep quickly in order to capture the loveliness of the moment.

Your coming was late compared to your mother. Your mother arrived on our second wedding anniversary, a double blessing. She joined her older (by only fourteen months) brother and took her place in our family. Throughout all her growing years I hoped that one day she too would know the joy, the absolute joy of motherhood and the delights of a having a daughter.

I remember when your mom and dad told us of your pending arrival. We celebrated with hugs and tears. I had all I could do not to say "it's about time!" I shared those months of your being within your mom. She and I would talk about you and about our hopes for a healthy, happy baby. We never mentioned that we would prefer one sex or the other, we were just delighted that you were on your way.

Finally the day arrived. You were about to be born and grandpa and I went to the hospital to be with your mom and dad for a few minutes. When we left your mom promised that she would call as soon as you were born. I lay in bed that night remembering when our daughter was born, remembering as only the mother could remember the feelings both physical and emotional that are present during those hours. Try as I may sleep eluded me for most of the night and finally just when I thought I could stand it no longer, the phone rang.

"Mom, mom it's me. There is a baby girl here who would like to meet you." "Oh darling, are you ok, is the baby ok?" "Yes mom we are but can you come quickly, she is waiting for you." By now your grandfather was wide awake and greeted the news with a big smile. "We are on our way." I phoned the great grandparents and quickly departed for the hospital. It was early morning, the last faint image of the moon hung in the sky, the birds were beginning their morning concert and I too sang within my heart and my soul. You were here and that's all that mattered.

When I arrived at the doorway of the room that held you and your mom and dad the tears began to flow. I glanced at the new mother cradling her newborn daughter gently in her arms, the daddy looking adoringly at both.

You have been named Elisabeth Adrian, what a lovely sound and I repeat the sounds to those who will listen. Your arrival helps to complete the circle of life, the extension of family. You have come at a time with the expectation of God's promise.

Everyone told me that grandchildren are special. I thought perhaps that might be so and waited patiently (well, sort of patiently) for the word that a grandchild was on the way. I guess I was anxious to have a grandchild and hoping that the event would happen at the same time determined to keep my mouth shut. For me having children was, as the kids today would say, awesome and I hoped my children would feel the same way.

When we leave the hospital and return home I go immediately to the desk and remove a folded, wrinkled piece of paper. On it I had written a poem right after I gave birth to my first child. I never finished it and I am not sure why. It was placed in a book in a drawer there to remain until today. It is now time to finish it.

> Long before you were to be I loved you
> and it was just you and me.
> I thought of you and held your smile
> that, of course, I could see for mile after mile.
>
> I cuddled and cooed and held you so tight,
> I loved you and wanted you with all of my might.
>
> When others would think nothing of this,
> I would hold you in my dreams and think only of a kiss.
> How would you look, how would it feel
> to be a mommy at last when the time became real?
>
> Others would plan and wait for the date,
> not me I ran head first toward you and your being.
> I ran for dear life, I ran toward your smile,
> I ran with a passion, that only I could explain.
>
> I ran toward the prayer and promise of love,
> I ran toward the gift sent to me from above.

October Sunshine

October Sunshine

October days in New Hampshire can be spectacular. The cool crisp air, clear blue skies, and the glorious colors of red, gold and yellows can lead to one of those "ain't it great to be alive feelings." Today was just that kind of day, a real New Hampshire autumn day. Back roads and local general stores filled with tourists out to see this spectacular display of nature. Children scurried through piles of leaves and there was a distinct autumn smell in the air.

The drive up through the Connecticut River Valley was an opportunity to reflect upon this beauty and other accruements of nature that reflected the changing seasons. Smoke wafting from the chimneys of family homesteads, corn husks bowing their brown sheaths to the ground like weary soldiers that could not go one more step, and evening dusk coming just that much sooner.

We awoke the next morning to the same sights and smell, the same colors and sky but the days activities were not to include a drive through country lanes or the taste of cider and donuts at a wooden stand or the sight of "snow" leaves just beginning to gently flutter to the ground. No, this day was to include things not experienced in my life , nor imagined in my soul. This day in all its beauty was to include the end of a life season and the changing of a son forever.

The call came early and the summons we had steeled ourselves to hear penetrated not only our ears, but our very hearts. "It's time, please come." The call had been expected and woke us from a fretful night of sleep. Showers, shaving and the usual morning routine had no place in this morning's activity. Instead we placed our bags in the car and drove quickly through the cool crisp dawn of another New Hampshire October morn. Words came but were punctuated by silences that themselves spoke volumes. By the time we arrived, the sun was beautiful in the sky. I took his hand as we approached the building.

We pushed open the door and were greeted by an elderly gentleman and lady talking quietly in the corner. "Good morning, how are you today?" we were asked. "Fine thank you," I replied and kept moving down the corridor. "*Fine thank you,*" I repeated to myself thinking of the absurdity of those words at this particular moment and yet the gentleness in which they were spoken.

We went directly to the office of the lady who had called us. She opened the door and asked us to take a seat. "This is a difficult time for you," she said and although you know she had had much experience with this, you could tell she still found it difficult. "I am so glad that you were able to come, he was looking forward to seeing you. He wanted to talk to you and tried so hard to wait for you, but I'm afraid that he won't be able to talk when you see him." "Not talk to us, why Pa could always talk to us. He could talk to anyone." From the day I first met him he never found it difficult to keep up a conversation.

She gently explained what changes had taken place and what we could expect when we saw him. "He may or may not recognize you but it is important to let him know you are here. He felt he had things his son had to hear and he could not die without those things being said. Do you think you are ready to go upstairs now?"

We both nodded and quietly followed her to the elevator. I was trying to think of something to say but instead felt it proper to just keep silent. As we approached the room a nurse was coming out. She looked into our faces, smiled gently and moved aside for us to enter. The curtains had been drawn and the lights dimmed. The room reminded me of the evening when the sun had gone down and the lights needed to be turned on. It was almost as though we were in shadows as we entered.

We moved toward the bed and looked upon the figure lying on his side. Reaching for his hand I bent close so he could see me. His son, on the other side of the bed, did the same.

"Hello Pa, we are here. We've come to be with you." He stared straight ahead and then as if his mind awakened, he moved his eyes toward his son. For a moment they stared at each other, hand in hand, and heart in heart. There was no movement from his limbs. They remained just as they were. But his eyes, they moved and searched and spoke the unspoken words.

"We love you Pa, we love you very much. Your children and grandchildren all love you. You were a good father, you brought us joy." And so we talked, son to father, wife to husband, wife to father. Words that could only be spoken one way, answers that would come no longer. We spent hours like this just the three of us. Hours that included songs, tales of long ago, happenings of today, adventures of tomorrow and as the time shortened, I explained about the glorious day.

"It is just your kind of day Pa, the kind of day you reveled in on your farm. The sky is so blue and look, look at the colors of the trees." We gently lifted him in our arms and moved the curtains so the sun streamed in on his face. Tree branches tapped gently at the window and leaves fell silently to the ground. For a moment he looked straight at the sun, then the sky and finally the leaves. Afterwards, we placed him gently back on the pillow.

I am not sure how long after that it was that he was gone, but as he left us his face shone with the beautiful, bright sunshine of a fine New Hampshire day. It was just his kind of day, a day to ride off into the sun and experience the beauty that was the changing of the seasons.

October Mist

October Mist

It was to be almost a week before we would once again be in the presence of Pa. This time we were keenly aware of the changes that had taken place in the past week and so steeled ourselves to recognize those changes and to bring to completion this part of his life.

Once again it was a beautiful October day as we set out to travel the highways and back roads that would take us to our emotional destination. We were to gather in New Hampshire, children, grandchildren and friends to pay as the phrase goes, "our last respects."

On the way we were to stop in a small town and pick up the ashes. How strange I thought as I rode along sharing everyday thoughts and feelings with my parents and husband. We spoke of the lovely weather, the gorgeous colors of the foliage, the traffic and much more of the small talk that seems to help pass the time especially when some words may seem awkward and uneasy to speak. It does not seem real this journey; this life changing journey that would mark forever the passing of one generation and the changing of another.

As we approached the funeral home where we would meet with the funeral director and receive Pa's ashes, I noticed how quiet my husband had become. "Can you please go in and get the ashes for me," he asked. "I don't think I can do this." "Of course I will," I answered as I reached for his hand noticing the beginnings of tears filling his eyes. My heart ached for this son who now would gather his dad, his Pa, and return him at last to his beloved farm. It is what Pa wanted, to be cremated and his ashes spread on his land among the pine trees and berry bushes that had been his life and love for so many years.

"Just wait in the car and I'll be right back. I wish I knew what to say to you but somehow I can't find the words." Turning from the car I approached the funeral home while I too held back tears. The funeral director was pleasant and spent a few minutes talking about the package I was to pick up. He told me how the ashes would look and how to go about spreading them. And then he told me to wait there and he would be right back. If minutes seemed like hours it was then. Could I do this without breaking down? Would I be able to be of strength for my husband? How do you carry what was left of a life you had known and loved in your hands?

The blue box was placed on the desk while the director asked me if I was OK. He came around, helped me from my chair and I took possession of this fragile, emotion filled package. Thanking him I left the home and approached the car. I noticed that my husband was not looking in my direction nor making any attempt to come toward me. Mom opened the back door and Pa and I got in.

This time as we rode toward Pa's town the words were few and the silences more pronounced.

I placed the box on the floor between mom and I and rode along in my own reverie. Our next destination was the florist and finally the priest to make final preparations for the service.

At last the preparations were over and we headed to a bed and breakfast that would provide shelter for us that evening. We approached the large white frame house by way of a winding dirt road. The house sat on a knoll at the bend of the road just after crossing a small wooden bridge that creaked with age and use.

Upon the arrival of the children that evening, the place took on a feeling of normalcy. Quickly the bantering began. "Hey, I'll take this room." "Mom, did we bring shampoo?" "I'm not sleeping with anyone who snores." The sounds of this bantering brought back memories of family vacations and precious time spent in common everyday conversations and for that I was grateful. As we settled in for the night I moved from room to room and child to child, now in or approaching adulthood and spent time in quiet reflection with each one.

The two older boys spent time talking about their summers, year after year on the farm with Pa. Our daughter wondered how tomorrow would go. The youngest cried. We embraced and settled down for the night. I climbed in next to my husband and finally fell asleep after lying awake for what seemed like hours listening to the sounds that only stillness in the country can bring.

Dawn broke and everyone prepared for the day. This was to be an emotional day for all. We carefully bridged our words and the children made every effort to be as close to their dad as possible both in a physical way and I am sure in a spiritual way. I took care of Pa and made sure he too took his place in the car.

Upon arrival at the church, I walked down the aisle with the blue box in hand and carefully placed Pa on a small wooden table that was covered in a white linen cloth. The organ began to play and people began to arrive. There in front was the basket of beautiful fall flowers part of a memorial but a reminder of Pa's garden. I listened as the mass began, the music played while the tears seeped from our eyes.

It was a lovely service full of meaning and dignity. The priest spoke about the changing seasons in nature and in human life, the son eloquently spoke of Pa's life and I read from a children's story that explained death in gentle words. Folks in the congregation rose and talked about Pa and what he meant to them.

Afterwards we all proceeded to the farm to bring Pa home. The small caravan wound over the roads, past the river, the general store and finally into the driveway of the farm. As we approached our destination the sun seemed to disappear and rain clouds began to be visible on the mountains. We drew our garments to ourselves and walked toward the field, some walking alone, others holding hands or with arms entwined.

Because I was carrying the box of ashes I led the way and choose the place where Pa at last would rest. I knelt in the crumpled leaves and carefully opened the blue box. As the priest read from the Book of Prayers and as tears flowed freely from family and friends, I carefully placed his ashes on the ground.

Although his son stood close by me I was only aware at that

moment of one person, Pa. "Please bring me home," he so frequently asked during those last few months. "Please bring me home." Now my tears flowed too and I was aware of a fine mist that gently fell to the ground. "You are home now Pa, we love you and will miss you but at last you are home."

As the small band of family and friends took leave from the sacred spot the October mist continued to fall gently to the ground covering the barren bushes and the newly laid ashes.

Barren Branches

Barren Branches

On a cool crisp October evening just as the sun was setting in the purple sky, once more we gathered with family and friends to bid farewell to Pa. This time the ceremony was held hundreds of miles from his beloved farm and in a setting not familiar to him. This time the church was larger and the congregation made up of those people that somehow were involved more with the lives of his son and grandchildren but not necessarily known to Pa. To be sure there were some of his family members, those too old and frail, or too busy to have traveled the distance to visit him in the previous months, co-workers and nieces, nephews and such.

The service while almost a repeat of the earlier one included prayers from a priest, eloquent moving words from a son still numb with his loss, the reading of the gentle words from the children's book and the reflections on his life offered from the congregation offered noticeable differences as well.

These were not the "folks" from his beloved New Hampshire, those who came often to the farm just to "shoot the breeze" or pick the berries or deliver another load of fertilizer and then stay to discuss the weather and the crops. These were the people of his life in years away from the farm. This time also there was the addition of a very special someone, his only great grand child who would refer to him throughout her life as the great grandpa I never knew. This precious representative of life itself arrived for the ceremony nestled in the arms of her mother and at times lent an almost lightheartedness to the evening. It was during the lighting of the candles on the alter that we were to hear the innocent voice of a child singing her rendition of the happy birthday song.

And there were other noticeable differences. This time there were no flowers on the alter and no blue box. What was left of Pa's ashes remained behind in our home for placement at a later time next to his wife and daughter. On the small, linen covered table we had placed a vase containing branches taken from his berry bushes on the farm. These barren branches represented to us not only his death, but the deeper meaning of his life, his vigil in the fields from the time of the barren branches in winter to their budding in the spring, the ripening fruit bending the branches in summer, the turning of the leaves in the autumn and once more the barren branches themselves.

Almost two weeks had passed and we, Pa's children and grandchildren had begun to resume our normal lives. Our days were now filled with work and school, rather than preparations for burial ceremonies. There were to remain a few more beautiful October sunshine days but the magnificent colors of New England foliage were rapidly disappearing, replaced instead with gray skies and crumpled leaves and memories of a lifetime carried within our hearts. Pa's life on earth was gone, his days with us over, but as sure as spring would arrive again, we would return to his beloved farm and to his world. Our pilgrimage always began in the spring when once more we would be welcomed by the barren branches, so soon to bud and bloom again.

Coming And Going

Coming and Going

Sitting close together that evening, Mom and I were to share an experience that would change us and our understanding of life. We had been there for hours, in fact for days existing in that twilight that you experience when you are not asleep and not quite awake. In those hours what is real may seem unreal and what is unreal may seem to be real.

There were periods of normal conversation where we discussed weather, jobs, the economy and all those topics that may or may not be interesting but serve a useful purpose to break uneasy silences. These short dialogs were then followed by longer periods when both of us would retreat into our own thoughts and conversations.

Time was measured in brief interludes when we were notified that we could go in to see dad for the ten minutes per hour that you were allowed. We took turns, mom and I holding his hand, touching his face and gently prodding him to move away from the death that was hovering so close by him and to hang on to life. He responded weakly to these suggestions and only briefly would show that his body still craved life. His speech was difficult and measured by the restriction of his oxygen mask.

Looking down at him in this sterile hospital environment I felt sadness and fright. This was dad, my daddy and I, inside of me still his little girl needed him, wanted him and would do all in my power to keep him. These brief interludes became treasured moments and yet filled with deep pain and fright. Dad was slipping away and we in all our effort could only stand by with silent prayers and gentle caresses. "Dad," I repeated over and over again. "You need to hang on and get better, you have someone special waiting just for you." He looked into my eyes and I think we both saw the hint of tears on our cheeks.

A life was ending or so we thought and yet the power and pull of life was also evident in that place. We continued to talk to him about the miracle that was taking place just yards away from him and the part that he was to play in this tiny life. "They tell us the baby is due any moment now. I wonder if it will be a boy or a girl. Isn't it exciting daddy?"

Not far away from this valley of death was another place where a life struggled to come into being. When we could mom and I, holding hands would move toward the brightness of that holy place. We would quietly tiptoe toward the door, silently push it open and see her on the bed. There lying in another hospital bed was my daughter preparing for the miracle in which she was taking part.

All around her were the items that spoke of life. In place of an oxygen mask was the fetal monitor. The rhythmic sound spoke to us of the tiny life just out of our view that was to come and in those sounds we took comfort from the child who relayed to us the message of life. In place of gauze dressings were tiny articles of clothing and in place of a crash cart was the warming bassinet prepared to hold the new born.

Hour after hour we moved from the darkness to the light all the while experiencing the deepest sadness and the greatest joy. Would dad live long enough to see his new great grandchild, would the baby come in time? "My God," I thought, "this does not make sense to me." I needed to somehow make sense of what was happening and struggled with my emotions.

While we passed the hours in this manner, nature and energy itself was changing. The darkest night sky gently transformed itself into a beautiful sunrise. Birds could be heard singing outside of the window and the bustle of activity was evident throughout the building. Then the call came for us to return to the area of "life." We again quietly tiptoed toward the door, and pushed it open. This time mom and I moved toward the bed and there, lying in her mothers arms, was life itself.

We stood, four generations together in those first precious moments when time itself seems to stand still. And then as if she knew, the tiny hand curled around ours and the face looked to us. "Sarah," I cooed, "my beautiful Sarah, you have come in time." My daughter held the child out to mom as though she knew that mom needed to feel life, needed to touch the warmth and newness and joy.

After some time we left the area of life and moved once more to the area of darkness. As we moved toward ICU, I held mom's hand a little tighter and drew her to me. "Don't worry" she said, "it's going to be alright, you'll see."

When we arrived, the nurse met us at the door. "I'm glad you are here, there has been a change, you may want to go to your husband." I let mom lead the way since I was too afraid of what I might see and not prepared for what I might hear. We quietly tiptoed toward the door, and pushed it open and there on the bed lay dad, his face peaceful and with a hint of a smile. My legs were like rubber and the weight of my chest was suffocating.

As we approached the bed dad struggled to turn his head to look into our faces. "Well," he asked, straining for each word, "well, what do we have?" "It's a girl daddy and she is so beautiful, just wait till you see her." Once again the tears came, once again I held this frail hand but this time, this time I knew that it would be different. Dad had hung on, reached for life, struggled for it just as the child had, fought through the night into the newness of the day. My heart leapt for joy.

As we were leaving the ICU unit, mom pushed open the door, almost bumping into someone. "Excuse me", she said, "I'm sorry." "Are you coming or going?" The lady replied, "I'm coming." With a smile on her face and a twinkle in her eye, mom replied, "we're coming too, we're all coming."

Flower Pots

Flower Pots

On my way to work one morning they appear as if out of nowhere. I look to the right and there they are. I know instinctively that when I am not looking they appear as if someone steals in the darkest of night and places them there for me to see in the morning. These harbingers of autumn appear for only one reason, to remind me of the quick passing of time.

One moment the field is bare except for the green of the trees surrounding it and the blacktop of the adjacent roadway. First comes the black plastic laid out as a mantle covering the place where green meadows and wild flowers should be. It wouldn't be so bad if this field took on the appearance of the one to the left of the nursery where row upon row of spring and summer flowers and shrubs greet the passerby with the news that indeed spring has arrived.

No, this field is to bring the messengers of autumn, fall, cool weather and the sure uneasy knowledge that once more winter will arrive. As I pass this field and this signal of autumn I try to figure out why such a commonplace natural occurrence would bother me so much. Why in heaven's name would the planting of chrysanthemums in pot after pot, row after row have such a profound affect on me?

"It's only flowers; it's only someone planting flowers," I repeat over and over again. Yet my very soul tells me that as beautiful as they are, they trigger this feeling of sadness. Am I like Dad I wonder who from my earliest recollection would indicate to me by his words that spring and summer would pass ever so quickly and the sheath of fall and winter would once again settle all around us?

Dad would enjoy the 4th of July at the lake or on a picnic in the yard but never let us forget, "That's it, summer is over." As a child this made no sense to me. School was just about out and the long hot glorious days of endless summer were about to begin. Dad had other reminders of fall and winter as well. Woe to anyone who pointed out hydrangeas in bloom. That was just another omen that for sure winter was just around the corner.

Time and again Dad would remind me in one way or another that although you may catch a fleeting glance of happiness that always, just around the corner would come something to take away the good feelings of joy and happiness and replace it with a more somber mood. It was not for me to understand as a child, I didn't try and dad (or mom) made no effort to explain. It's just how it was.

And so I didn't pursue this attitude of dad's. I guess I too just assumed it's just how it was. I do recall that I recognized that a part of this would shape my being as well. Spring and summer would arrive, long delightful days, beautiful flowers, picnics, vacations and so very much more. And then fall would arrive stealing into our lives sometime when I was sleeping. Although there were pumpkins to select from a farmer's field, and colorful leaves to bring home and save by pressing them between sheets of waxed paper, there was always a feeling almost mournful that crept in.

Through the years of my youth I tried to understand just how and why this mournful feeling tiptoed into our home.

Although dad talked a lot about his father, I did not know till many years had passed that in was in the winter of his 14th year that dad lost grandpa. What a profound affect it had on him. How it colored his life and contributed to such a deep sadness within. I would learn years later how grandpa became so sick in the fall and finally passed away in the dark days of winter.

To add to my confusion, when I was growing up I did not have anything lavender or purple articles of clothing, nor did mom. I was told that dad did not like the color and again just assumed that's how it was. We had no shades of violet or purple anywhere, no linens, no colors on walls, no fabrics, nothing. Personally I always thought it was a pretty color but knew well enough not to press the issue. I would again in later years learn the reason why.

Grandmother had worn purple to the funeral and dad always associated purple with death.

Now that I am older I realize we probably all have "triggers" something that sets off a memory long buried. In this day and age the norm would be to bring it up, talk it out and "work on it." This is the age of therapy; self help groups, books in every size and shape that provide guidelines for improving your mental state. But dad and mom came from a different generation one where things were not discussed openly. Folks back then would just grit their teeth and bear it.

Several months after I had married I purchased a purple outfit. It was a lovely shade of violet and looked quite nice on me. I wore it home to see dad. He looked at me, held out his arms and gathered me to his chest. I remember his words, "You look lovely my daughter." I waited for the comment about the purple; I wondered why he did not mention it.

Over the years purple has shown up in lots of places in our lives, walls were painted, clothing was worn, and bunches of hydrangeas appeared on our table. I don't quite know if dad choose not to comment or had he finally reconciled himself to me having a home of my own with my own selections. I often wondered if it bothered him when he visited but I think my question was answered one Easter in early spring. Our new daughter was dressed in lavender. A cute, bubbly happy baby girl of five months. She held our her arms for her grandpa. He reached for her, and both of them laughed as he lifted her into the air. In picking her up, her little lavender dress had gotten wrinkled. With a careful hand he smoothed the wrinkles and said, "What a pretty dress you have, you are grandpa's beautiful girl."

I think perhaps dad could at last leave behind the sadness, the remembrance of purple and "those" flowers and look instead to this baby and a new way to look at the shades of life.

There's Always "Hope"

There's Always "Hope"

Week One

It has been just one week and the numbing feeling of last Wednesday is still very much a part of me, buried deep within my soul with no "exit" sign evident. I've been through this before with other things in life, the uncertainty, the disbelief, the questioning, all of it, and I don't want it again. I just want things to be OK. I want to make the world look and feel comfortable for me; I want the "sameness", to be there. I just want all this change to go away. "It's OK for the young ones", I say, "but not for me. Just leave me alone and let me do my job."

Corporate merger and downsizing, that's what this is all about. Corporate merger and change. I keep thinking I would feel different if it were my idea, you know, the whole thing, and the damn merger. But it is not my idea. It is theirs and the only thing I can do is react.

So once again I go to the bookshelf and stare at the books. You know, all those "Pick Yourself Up, Dust Yourself Off and Start All Over Again" books. There are religious books and psychology books, poems, stories, and autobiographies, hardbacks, pocketbooks, small, tall, brand new and some frayed with time and use. All aimed at one thing, how to cope and to change, how to make the best of it and grow yourself. "Hell," I think to myself.

The other thing I do is talk. I talk to my husband, talk to my children, call friends and say, "guess what, I do not have a job." It seems that I have a need to let everyone know that I have been rejected, that I do not fit into the new organization, that all I do is not really important. I have lost my sense of who I am in the workplace. How could they just come in and say my job is eliminated?

And then the reason side of me says, "Of course they can do what ever they want to do. The ball is in their court and they have the last volley. I can only react to what is happening and to those around me who are faced with the same situation. But darn it, everyone around me is young and as we know that's going to make a difference in the outcome."

Week Two

Life continues to move along, engines chugging toward the tunnel ahead, the darkness and uncertainty. Because I have been given a few months to find a new job, I continue to tell myself that life is OK and that I am going to be fine. And the "sameness" that I want is really here. And so it is, the sameness of the ride to work, the desk, the people, all the same. So for now I hang onto the sameness of each day knowing that somewhere in my gut I must really prepare for the inevitable relinquishing of the "sameness" and the preparing for the reorganization to come.

Week Three

I am surrounded by people who reach out to me; friends, family and co-workers who share their concern for me and for that I am grateful. I tell myself that I am not alone in this. There are so many others whose lives have been disrupted and torn apart. But for now I think only of me, of my life and my deep concern for my job.

My resume has been updated. I question it. Does it look good? Does it do me justice? Does it really tell the world who I am and what I can do? Will it get me a job? Hell, will it get me an interview? I put the dates on it, college, jobs, etc. Should I include the dates? Does it represent me and who I really am and what I am capable of doing?

I want the world to know me. "Please world, go gently with me and I will give you all I have. Stop, look and listen to me. I can do so much and I can be an asset to your organization. Please give me a chance."

Week Four

Hope calls me tonight. She calls to inquire about my job search and to let me know she is thinking of me. A special little old lady, someone I hardly know, someone confined to a wheelchair in a convalescent home calls me. I feel blessed.

She tells me about who she has contacted on my behalf—who she wants to inform about this "wonderful lady with so much to offer and who would certainly be an asset to any organization." Hope is determined to help me in my job quest. "Do stop by with your resume so I can pass it along and set up some interviews."

"Well," I say to myself, "Hope is on the job, what more do I need?"

Week Five

The tears have subsided somewhat and sleep comes easier. In fact, I seem to be sleeping more, a first for me. At the sound of the alarm I just roll over and pull the covers higher. It is hard to go into the office day after day and face the reality of it all. I am even tired of writing in my journal.

Week six

Now the dreams have begun. So far, there is some humor to these dreams. One night I am on the lawn of the White House waiting for an interview with President Clinton. I keep saying that I don't want to meet him, I don't even like him but I am spurred on to the interview. My husband keeps telling me, "Don't bother with the low level positions, go for the top."

Co-workers have begun to be called for interviews but there is still no action for me. I begin to question why I have not been called for an interview when I have put so much of me into the job. Is it my age? Did the dates on my resume limit my chances? "I told you so, this is going to be harder for you than for the young co-workers in the office."

Week seven

Today I change my resume and submit it again minus my teaching and education positions. Leave them off even though it shows that I did something important and valuable outside of this company. Leave them off because of the dates. Leave off the wonderful talent I have for working with varied age groups. Leave off all the information about kindergarten teaching, subbing, curriculum development for young children. I have now been in the corporate world long enough that perhaps that background does not matter any more.

"Hey toots, you are getting off track," I say to myself.

Week eight

I have vacation and personal time left from last year. I need to take it or I will loose it. I do not feel like going away. Not until something is definite with my job situation. Once I am settled again I aim to take a long trip. I am one of those people who put off treating myself. I keep telling myself "Someday you will be able to travel, to go to England and spend time in the ancestral country of my dreams." For all I know the time may be now.

This week I do not want to talk. I do not want people to stop by and ask me how I am doing. I do want people to pat me on the back and tell me I will be fine. Go away I silently scream, go away and leave me alone. Today I am reviewing my life and I am discouraged at what I have not accomplished.

Week nine

Interviews have been going on and so far none for me. How do I feel about this? I'm not really sure. Part of me is discouraged and wondering if I'll ever get an interview. Part of me is resigned that it may take a little longer for me. I tell myself that something more suitable is in store and that I am going to be fine. I'm being selected for something even better than the job I have now. Just wait till the dust settles!

Do I believe this or am I fooling myself? Again I question my resume. Does it do me justice? Is it written according to the guidelines we were given? Should I submit it again? This is all new to me. Previously, I just mailed my resume but this, this new on-line procedure is very different. Did I include the correct buzzwords to be scanned?

Although my main emphasis has been to remain with this company for retirement reasons, I am now stepping up my efforts in the outside world to see what I find there.

Week ten

Again I question my resume. Does it do me justice? Is it written according to the guidelines we were given? Should I submit it again to the automated system?

There is clearly no way to hide my age. There is no way to look thirty or thirty-five again. God where did the time go? I wonder if these young people that surround me really have a clue to how fast time goes. I don't think they do. I certainly did not at that age. I was too busy with life to even contemplate the rapidness in which our lives go.

I want to preach to them and tell them to be sure to do everything they want to do and not to put things off too long. But will they listen?

"Hey kid, you're getting off track again. Just keep to yourself and your problem. There is no need to worry about everyone else. You have enough to do to just get a job."

Week eleven

This week I go to the convalescent home to see Hope. Why didn't I go sooner to see this lovely, kind and caring lady? Am I so busy with my problems that I do not or cannot focus on others?

As I walk down the long corridor I can see Hope in her wheel chair and when she finally sees me, she is delighted. At last I have come to see her. She can't wait to talk to me and find out all about my job search. "Come," she says, "Let's go to my room where we can talk. I want to hear all about how things are going for you."

She tells me about her contacts and ensures me that she will continue to do as much as she can for me. "You are just the kind of person that anyone would want to work for, you have so much to offer."

"Thank you," I silently repeat to myself, "thank you for thinking about me."

Now I just need others in the corporate world to think that way too.

Week twelve

It is hard to believe it has been almost three months since all this began. Looking back it confirms my observation that life continues to move along so very swiftly and the current seems to carry us faster as we grow older. I cling to the hope of getting a position that I will like just as one clings to a raft moving through the rapids. When you are on the raft there is little you alone can do to move the raft safely through those rapids.

Daily we hear the news about positions that have been filled and I rejoice for those who have accepted a job. The others who are left still struggle with, "will I get an interview, will I get a job?"

Tuesday I am notified that I have been chosen for an interview. "At last," I tell myself, "someone wants to talk to me."

Wednesday I dress the part, I mentally prepare for the interview. I will bring materials to show what I have done in my current job and answer the standard questions. I am relaxed and that is good. After the interview I feel elated. The interview went very well and I have hope.

Friday I receive a call to inform me that I did not get the job. Oh, I am told that I am very qualified but not just the right candidate. I want to cry, I am sad. Well, maybe not sad but resigned that this process will take longer than I had hoped and resigned that the playing field is full of qualified players and this game will be a hard one to call.

My days and nights continue to be anxious. I am overeating, oversleeping, overanxious and over concerned that I keep repeating to myself, "Oh God, when will this end and how will it end?"

"Just shut off your computer and go home. It's time to quit for today."

Week thirteen

One by one my colleagues are receiving word that they have been selected for a job either in the new organization or have found employment in a new company. One my one they come by and tell me and I extend my congratulations. One by one they are preparing to leave. One by one I watch and listen.

My mind is racing with the words, "What's wrong with me? Where are all the interviews? What will happen to me?"

True, I have been contacted by outside companies and I have responded to some ads. I wait and wonder...

I sit at my computer but words do not come easily. Maybe this writing down of my thoughts should be put aside for a time. I decide not to finish my journal entries.

Later

Time passes. I have been employed now for quite a while in a new company and loving it. I am in charge of a department, we are doing great things. Oh how wonderful I think. All the pain and uncertainty is behind me, no need I tell myself to continue the journal. By now the story is old, the frustrations and anxiety not as raw and cutting to my being. At last I am on track. I have a future again, security and the good old American paycheck and 401K. I can sleep at night. I can plan for my trip. I can go and visit Hope.

More time has passed. Weeks, months, a year. Today I receive a call from my daughter. She is crying. "Mom, Hope died."

There is a tightening in my throat and I fill up with tears. I have been so busy with a new job in a new company surrounded by new co-workers I seldom had the time (or so I thought) to think of Hope or to visit her. Once in a while on my way home I would think of her. "Tomorrow", I would tell myself, "tomorrow or on the weekend I would stop by. Hope will be there. There is always hope."

Weeks, months, and gradually the excitement of the new job turns to uncertainty. Once again I am to feel the ending of a job and the beginning of a search process. Once again I hear the words, "I am sorry to have to tell you this...."

I run home to my desk. Where is my journal? I need to write down all these feelings, I need to finish the entries, I need to get rid of this pain, this sorrow. Can this be happening again to me? I am quietly reminded of a small, frail lady, confined to a wheelchair. "Don't' worry my dear," her words ring in my ears, "Remember there is always hope."

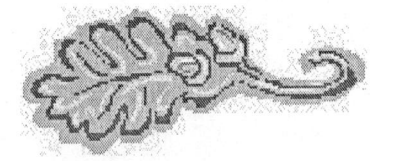

The Builder

The Builder

Genes are a wonderful thing. They determine how we look, what color our skin is, how tall we will be, the color of our eyes, and more. But I am convinced that genes also pass from one generation to another the "hard to define" uniqueness of each person.

Take for example our youngest son, the builder, inventor, fixer, mechanic, and tinker. How could this child have known even in his beginning years that his two great grandfathers deceased before his birth and paternal grandfather were the same? How could this child who stole away time and again to his tiny workbench know how to start such a project, how to manipulate things, how to form things, how to make "things" so early in life? As the tiny child grew so grew his projects.

It was not unusual to see him remove himself from others and turn to his venture. He would sometimes draw plans but most often the plan was in his head and all he needed was time and materials. "Just like grandpa," we would say. Whenever he was missing we would know just where to find him. Bent over the work area, little hands sawing, gluing, measuring, until, with the look of a fine master craftsman, he would present us with his achievement. I do not recall ever having to ask him what it was.

Through the years this attribute was demonstrated in many ways, in happy times and even when life seemed overwhelming to him. "A man of few words," people would say. But oh how he spoke with his hands! There were the miniature lanterns made from tiny glass model paint jars, pieces of string, and the littlest handle to turn the string wick made from a wire hanger. In all, the working lantern stood just barely two inches tall.

He made wonderful bird houses like the ones found in upscale garden centers, fancy boxes, models and so much more. With each project he developed his technique until at last his work was of the finest quality. One time he made a very impressive chess set from bits of ceramic tile and automobile engine parts fashioned into the chess pieces. The edge was finished with several pieces of molding which he stained and polished. If you saw it you would think like I do—this could be sold in a specialty store on Fifth Avenue.

Some projects were the invention of a happy child delighted to produce something he made. Sometimes they reflected his deepest emotions, his sorrow, his pain. It was not long after he was diagnosed with a life changing illness that he produced items associated with sadness. I do not think it proper to go into this but again it was his hands that showed us his pain. He worked quietly, alone, and in deep thought. I thought perhaps I should do something, but as I watched him I instinctively knew what he needed most was exactly what he was doing.

As time went by this child became a young man and true to form he continued his creating. It would be more "grown up" now, tearing engines apart, making shelves and book cases for his room, and when he finished his tradesman program as a tool maker he delighted us with a exceptional wooden tool chest, one of many he would fashion.

This young man then found the love of his life, a special girl who would appreciate and encourage his building. She would admire his work, and provide the time and space for him to build. When these two young people were to marry, Chris, without anyone knowing, created a tiny steel case including the screws to hold it and the tiny screw driver to open it. Inside was a grooved out space to hold the engagement ring he would carry half way around the world to his beloved who was finishing a summer abroad as an assistant archeologist in Greece.

The story goes that he waited for just the right moment, a moonlight evening, stars twinkling above and the Aegean Sea lapping at the shore. Chris removed the tiny screwdriver from its hiding place and proceeded to open the case. There was the ring, the symbol of love, the evening like one out of a romance novel.

This son, true to his character, spoke few words to us about what happened. Imagination told the story. In a few years he would marry and leave behind the vestiges of his building years in the family home. As he prepared his new home he set up his workbench, lathes, saws and other paraphernalia that were the genesis of his being. As luck would have it the home they purchased had an area just for such purpose.

On the day of the wedding he showed us what he had made to carry the rings to church. Why were we not surprised? They were a pair of matching metallic paper weights edged with brass. These handsome, one of a kind, cases opened, again with a tool he had made. Inside were the spaces to hold the rings. As I admired them I stole a glance at my son. A wide grin covered his face, he relished the compliments. He handed them to his brother the best man.

I am sure his bride knew that something made by her beloved would carry the rings to church. I am sure she saw the wide grin as they were opened during the ceremony. I am sure her heart beat just a little faster as she appreciated this unique present.

Will this trait be passed again to another generation? Will another child steel away to create, to huddle with wood? Will another child produce such unique objects, will another generation travel to a beach far away and under a moonlight sky bring forth a tiny container that held volumes?

Life Is Like A Profit And Loss Statement

Life is Like a Profit and Loss Statement

All we hear about today is the stock market, the seemingly unending downward spiral of people's life savings is spread across headlines in evening newspapers and reported on the lips of nightly newscasters. For months now the climate of the economy has changed. Gone are the days of riding the stock market to great heights and rewards. Gone are the day traders who cunningly and feverishly reported large earnings. Today people talk only of the loss of millions, perhaps billions of retirement savings.

I admit that I am not familiar enough with financial matters to begin to panic. For some reason I have confidence that in the end all will be well. Call it wishful thinking, immaturity, a sort of a hiding my head in the sand action. But I have come to the realization that life itself is like the stock market, one minute up and the other down. One day life is good, everything is working in sync to produce positive results and then wham! The "stock market of life" hits the skids.

I suppose that as a reasonably intelligent person I should pay more attention to the details offered on NPR or the evening news. I should perhaps call our brokerage house and speak to our financial experts. At the very least I should read the monthly statements that come in detailing the activity of the last month.

Quite often I tried to grasp the ins and outs and round abouts of the market. It was futile. All those men and women running around, pen and pad in hand reaching and yelling to whomever made no sense to me. Why I was raised in a home where money was tight and the only transactions I could see was mom counting the money dad brought home in an envelope once a week. She would sit at the dining room table and the place the money into little piles—one for food, one for utilities, one for gas for the car, one for oil for our two second floor stoves.

I truly cannot remember ever hearing her say, "This goes into the stock market, or I'm going to put this into investments." In our house an investment did not exist. No one spoke of their stocks, bonds, and mutual funds. An investment in our house was a coat big enough when you bought it could last for several growing years. Why I cannot even remember a check book or a savings statement.

Relatives of ours did buy stocks and had savings accounts. I never knew that until later. Growing up I just thought everyone got paid in cash, sat at the dining room table and made little piles. Today if I listen to some financial experts that just happen to be on the radio they will say, "If you save as little as $20.00 a week you will have so much in savings when you retire. I grab my son, the one still at home and lecture him, "Did you know that if you save as little as $20.00 a week you will have so much in savings when you retire?"

"Mom, for God's sake, I have CD's, bonds and I'm already in the stock market." Can this be my child? Where have I been and what have I been doing? Who taught him this?

Mom and dad just sort of lived life each day and somehow everything always turned out. They didn't take fancy trips, nor wear fancy clothes. But we had good food, delightful family vacations and happy Christmas mornings. Except for the good food I'll bet there are rich people who do not have delightful family vacations and happy Christmas mornings. Today we probably would be living below the national poverty line.

"OK," I say to myself, "It's time to change." From now on you are going to become more involved in the financial picture. You are going to call the brokerage house, subscribe to *Money Management* and generally become more knowledgeable. I call my daughter and ask her if they are in the market. "Of course mom, we've been in the market every since we married, as a matter of fact, the girls are in the market too." Now I am really in trouble, what will the kids think of me if I don't know what's happening? How will I keep up with the grandchildren as they grow up? How will I keep from looking like a complete idiot when in the company of others someone begins to talk the talk I don't even understand?

But then I stop myself. I'm not really interested. I like my Profit and Loss statement better, it makes more sense. On the profit side I count my husband, my children, grandchildren and dear friends, etc. On the loss side I count the loss of my dad and all those whose lives are no longer physically entwined with mine. I truly believe things will turn out ok and I go on that premise. A fool I might be called and so what, at least I'm not sitting in front of a computer screen checking the index and reading reports from top brokerage firms. Instead I am sitting at a computer writing my book. It's a lot more fun and no one is running around with a pen and pad yelling at me. No one is telling me to update my portfolio, no one is making sure I am reading my profit and loss statement.

Ah, the joy of recklessness, the abandonment of worry, the fun of escaping the real world and sitting with myself wondering, contemplating, what would it be like to be into the market? For me I think I will clean off the dining room table and take stock of my life.

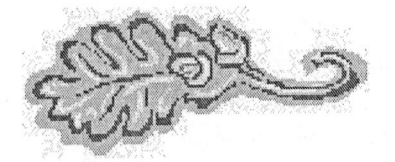

Neighbors

Neighbors

Yesterday I was in my backyard hanging a batch of laundry. As I placed them one by one on the line in just the right order I could feel a twinge of pride creeping into my person. Much like mom must have felt years ago standing on the back porch of our old Victorian home on the busy street called South Leonard Street. Yes, I thought, this is just how mom must have felt. I bent down to choose just the right article of clothing and placed it in just the right spot on the line.

All underwear, socks, blouses and shirts, pajamas and nightgowns, tablecloths and towels were arranged according to their function, size and color. Standing in the bright sunshine, barefoot with the greenest of grass tickling my toes, I reached into the laundry basket and, clothespin in hand, placed the articles on the line. Gosh I thought to myself, I am actually enjoying this domestic routine. Although the clothes line was not suspended from the second floor porch railing to the old garage roof, but was in fact, a newer portable clothes reel, I still felt a connection to a time long ago in a place so different from here.

I wondered how passer-bys would take to this scene. This is a neighborhood where one is not supposed to have an actual, real, honest to goodness clothesline suspended between trees or porches or garages. In this neighborhood none of the houses have clotheslines and very few have clothes reels. This is a neighborhood where clothes are dried in automatic dryers and never see the sunshine let alone any stranger's eyes. I don't feel offended if I happen to see someone's laundry on the line, mine included.

I am not passing judgment on those who choose to send laundry to the cleaners or to use an automatic dryer exclusively, no, not at all. What I am saying is that I am loving the connection to a time when doing the laundry meant an all day affair and represented a chance to impress the neighbors with a simple chore. I like how it feels in my hand, the touch of the dampness. I like how it looks hanging like soldiers on the line and most of all I like how it smells when you take in and fold it. Sorry, you just can't get that from a dryer no matter how much fancy smelling stuff you add to the wash.

A few years ago I had an antique booth set up next to a lady who exclusively sold antique linens. There set out on her table and hanging on old wooden clothes racks were the most beautiful starched and ironed linens you could imagine. She had lovely embroidered tea towels, matching table clothes and napkins, rows of crisp, white pillowcases trimmed with hand done lace, and other assorted pieces of cloth. I watched her open the containers and place the pieces in perfect order according to function, size and color.

As I was taking out my treasures to display on my table, I happened to take out a small wicker basket in the shape of a laundry basket. It was quite old and I believe had been part of a child's toy laundry set. When my neighbor saw it she immediately came over and picked it up. "Please save this for me, I will pay you before the day is over."

During the day I watched as one after another lady came to her table and ooh'd and aah'd over her linens. Comments like, "my grandmother had a table cloth like that." Or "do you remember sleeping at Aunt Jane's house, she always had perfectly ironed fancy pillowcases?"

Having grown up with lovely linens myself I was enjoying these comments. We might not have had a fancy house in an upscale neighborhood but we did have some nice linen that was passed down from generation to generation. They were used on special occasions only but they were there.

During a lull in the activity when fewer folks were stopping by our booths, I had the chance to talk with her. We discussed how much we loved to care for old linens. We commented that neither one of us found it a drudgery but in fact, found it to be relaxing. We both laughed when she said that she must have been a laundress in her past life and then told me that her mom had been a laundress for a family in her native France. I told her about a magazine article I read recently about a laundry in Europe that is still famous for exquisitely caring for family heirloom linens.

Later in the day, true to her word, my neighbor paid me for the basket and smiled as she walked away.

I packed my wares and went home. As tired as I was I went to find my box of antique tea towels. I took them out, counted them, and decided to find a way to display them. So now here they are all starched and ironed and ready for use by family and guests. Maybe some of them too had been lovingly cared for previously by a laundress in a fancy house long ago. But I know for sure they too had been hung out to dry on a line similar to mine and perhaps the owner of the towels hoped the neighbors would see them and smile or even offer a compliment.

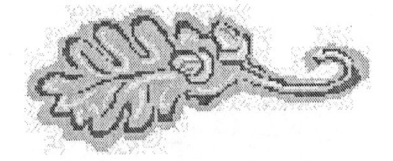

Waiting Rooms

WAITING ROOMS

Lately I have been spending a lot of time in waiting rooms. Because my parents are elderly with multiple health concerns and because my role is now that of caretaker I have the job of transporting them to doctor appointments, hospitals, labs, physical therapy offices and pharmacies. On our travels we see a wide range of "ologies" including oncology, hematology, cardiology, nephrology, ophthalmology, and so many more.

While I am there primarily to provide assistance for them I have found that this is a perfect place to observe life to the fullest. Since our family doctor is a "Family Practitioner" all ages are represented. First there is the couple coming in for a blood test, seated just out of sight of others and totally captivated by each other's glances. They are about to embark on a wonderful life journey and just cannot wait for it to happen. Oh, what I would like them to know about marriage! I would love to tell them all that I have learned through the years. I would tell them to overlook much, smile often, work through problems (work very hard), appreciate each other and allow each other to change and grow. I would tell them that even if they go to bed after a fight and they think they no longer like each other to always touch toes anyway. It helps.

Next comes the new mother with the new baby. She beams as she walks to the window to sign in and waits for the receptionist to coo and marvel over the child. Yes, her face is beaming, her walk light and happy. She carries a diaper bag filled with everything the child will need. Oh, what I would like her to know about babies, children and parenting! I would love to tell her all that I have learned through the years. I would tell her to watch the baby for all the special little things we sometimes miss, to enjoy each and every minute including nighttime feedings, soiled diapers, giggly sounds. I would tell her to really experience the first time the child smiles, holds her hand, and reaches for her face. I would tell her to love much, discipline wisely, hug often, sing and dance and run and play throughout all the early years. I would tell her to solicit warm gooey kisses.

Then comes the frazzled mother with her child in tow. She is here for a camp physical. She is about to launch her child into the realm of camp life. The child is excited; she seems to be a little preoccupied. This is a big step for both parent and child. Now someone else will be in charge, now someone else will hold responsibility for the welfare of the son or daughter. The child prances around the room showing off the new sneakers and shorts. He seeks out someone to talk to, someone who will listen as the story unfolds. "I am going to camp next week. I am going to sleep there too and learn how to paddle a canoe, ride a horse, and sleep in a tent."

Oh, what I would like her to know about children going to camp! I would love to tell her all that I have learned through the years. I would tell her pack extras of almost everything, to pack self addressed post cards and pens, to not worry about getting the names on everything (something is always missing anyway), to encourage the child to try everything, to remind them to be kind and gracious to fellow campers, to learn how to tip a canoe properly. I would also tell her to hug the child when it was time to leave but not to make the good-by take too long. I would tell her not to expect a post card but to be delighted if one comes.

Later a husband enters. I know he is a husband because of the wedding ring he wears. He is accompanied by a teenage girl who looks both disgusted and frightened. I wonder why the father is here and not the mother. The girl decides not to sit near the man and he is clearly agitated. What I wonder brings them here? I want to smile at them, a sort of motherly, wife like smile that hopefully would sooth the situation. They do not look up nor do they look at each other. Both wait in silence for the door to open and their name called.

Oh, what I would like them to know about teenagers and parents! I would love to tell them all that I have learned through the years. I would tell them how difficult it is to be either the parent or the child. I would tell them that this too would pass. I would tell them to talk things out, to not judge too easily, to be open to changes in generations, to love even when the going gets rough. I would tell them to go for ice cream after the appointment and to not skimp on the gooey stuff.

And then out of the corner of my eye I catch a glimpse of my parents. They are old and frail. That is obvious. They sit, dad resting his shriveled hands on his cane and just staring ahead as though he is deep in thought, mom rummaging once again through her purse for the appointment card she has just shown to the receptionist. My eyes see them, my heart sinks. How can this be? Where are my real parents? These people to be sure have some association to my parents but cannot be them. My parents are full of life, they laugh often. They take me to the doctor's office and buy me ice cream on the way home. It is they who worry about me, It is they who hold my hand and help me walk. It is they who listen intently to the doctor and get the information right the first time. It is they who administer the medicine to me, not me to them. Oh, what I would like them to know about me and them! I would love to tell them all that I have learned through the years.

I would tell them just how much I appreciate them, how much I love them. I would tell them to remember the words they have told me over and over again, "keep laughing, never give up, think about tomorrow and plan for each holiday." I would tell them thank you for all they have done. I would remind them once again about all of the wisdom they have given to me. I would tell them that I would be here for them just as they have always been there for me. I would tell them that I would hold their hand and take them for ice cream on the way home.

Thursdays are lab days. This waiting room is not so full and the waiting time prohibits even the picking up a of a magazine to read and hardly any time to watch and listen. This is only a brief stop, one where the outcome of the test (s) can only mean more trips to more doctors' waiting rooms.

On another day we are off to the hospital oncology waiting room. Here too the pattern of life is unfolding but with an urgency on one side and a quietness on the other. One after another the patients are called, blood is drawn and IV's prepared for treatment. The faces here tell a story of the fragileness of life, the hope and faith and so often the finality and the sorrow.

One by one they come, a middle-aged woman, turban on her head, holding the hand of a very worried husband. A young skinny bald headed man carrying college textbooks and accompanied by a beautiful, almost cheerleader type young lady. Here comes the widow who so desperately wants to tell someone, anyone about her Harry. They are all of us; we pray they are none of us.

Some people in waiting rooms become agitated if they are required to wait too long. They step up to the receptionist time and again letting her know just how long they have been here and how busy they are. "Do you know I have been waiting for at least 30 minutes?" one lady comments. The receptionist apologizes for the inconvenience. And the lady returns to her seat. Some people agree with her, some just turn away from her.

Life presents us with so many "waiting times." So many opportunities to sit and look and listen. Opportunities to contemplate our lives and those of the people we love. We have waited for joyous news such as the birth of a child. We have waited for the bus or train or plane that would bring home our loved one. We have waited for a change in someone at the edge of death. And yes, we have waited for the last breath that our loved one would take.

Waiting is so like life itself. A beginning, an end, and "stuff" in between. As we grow older so many people become more and more impatient. They almost feel that because they are now senior citizens they should not have to wait like other folks do. To these oldsters I say, "Waiting can be a great time—just wait and see."

She Only Came Once

She Only Came Once

One past year had been particularly difficult for me. In less than a year I was to experience herniated disks and the horrible pain that accompanied them, a week long bout of the flu in the winter, and a summer interrupted by a hospitalization for a bacterial infection that was to ravage my body and drain me in ways I could not have imagined. And to add insult to the list of injuries and ailments there were broken bones in my foot that came when at last I could return to work.

Each one of these afflictions would certainly have been enough. I was only in the first months of a new job when the accident occurred. On the advice of several doctors and with excruciating pain I had no choice but to remain at home for a period of time. It was during these very difficult days when I was truly wrestling with the deterioration of my body that I was struck with a more painful experience, one that would not be alleviated with just the taking of a pill.

Throughout my life whenever I had been injured or sick my mother was always there. She was my earliest playmate and it was she who soothed my soul, bandaged my cuts, removed slivers, made special treats when I was down with colds, measles, chickenpox and the like. She was my ride to the doctor and my constant companion, my comforter. She helped make tents in my sick bed, read stories and told me endless tales of long ago and of family from across the sea.

She came to me when I was afraid during the night, she held me when shots were administered, she removed lice from my hair and would climb the attic stairs to cuddle in my bed holding me when I was scared and telling me that everything would be all right.

Now when adult maladies caused me pain and anxious nights, now when visits to the hospital and doctors were mostly alone, now when I ached for her touch, her smile and hug, she only came once. I am sure she wanted to be with me, I am sure because I heard it in her voice and felt it in the unspoken connection between a mother and a child. But age and frailty prevented her from traveling just those few miles to administer the medicine of love.

As I lay in the hospital tethered to the IV tube in pain and distress, now when my body and soul ached for her touch, now when I needed her reassurance, now when the nakedness of body required her touch, now she only came once. It was the Wednesday of my hospitalization when she and dad appeared in the doorway. Dad had taken it upon himself to drive the few miles to bring her to me. How strange the visit—she approached my bed and caressed me and kissed my cheek. Her tiny arms held me, she looked into my eyes and I could see the words I needed to hear, "I'm here."

Sensing my need for reassurance she began to stroke my cheek, smooth my hair and feel my brow. Instantly I was transported back to the bed of my childhood. I allowed my thoughts to wander and my heart to rejoice.

Very soon though she needed to sit down and took her place beside dad. There they sat together, my parents, my mom and dad telling me stories and helping me to laugh. They told me that when I came home they would be there. "Don't worry honey, I'll be there and you can just rest."

When at last I was able to go home I was alone, mom and dad too frail and too tired to meet me. My connection to them was by phone and by heart only. My husband, my children and strangers brought soup and my only stories were those I read or wrote. Late one night when I needed her hug and kiss I called her on the phone. "Don't worry sweetheart, I'll have dad drive me tomorrow."

It was not that my husband, children and grandchildren were not attentive because they were. They were very attentive and came to see me daily in the hospital and when I came home they were all there holding my hand and asking what I needed. For that I am grateful. One cannot but remember a time when their mother played such a role. It seems as though the need for a mother is universal and the special bond that is formed while in the womb continues throughout our lives. We are told that on the battlefield wounded men will cry out not for their wives or girlfriends but for their mothers time and again.

It was like that for me. I wanted my mother. I think my longing was because I knew that both her and dad were becoming more frail and that as much as they wanted to care for me as they had for so many years the time of physical caring was over. That thought and the sight of them so frail and so in need of caring themselves brought home to me that one day they would be gone. Perhaps it was the pain, perhaps the events that happened one after another led me to become so sad and so in need.

But surprise me they did. Again dad took it upon himself to drive to my home and bring mom. They stumbled in the door needing assistance with the bundles they carried. Mom had a tasty rice pudding, a dish she alone makes to perfection. Dad came in with a bottle of ginger ale for my stomach. And of course, she brought all the articles she had cut from the newspaper, coupons for groceries when I felt better, and a blouse that perhaps I could use or pass to someone else. They stayed for a while and kept me company as I lay on the couch recuperating.

We laughed at some things and side stepped others. Soon the visit was over and they were gone. I remained on the couch for quite a while. I was sad. Their visit had been brief, their words calming, their lives and mine changed as only time and age can do. It has been years since that day, dad is gone and mom is here living with us. It is I now who care for her, I who stroke her head and hold her hand. I wonder sometimes if she is sad?

Old Kids

Old Kids

I have old kids. Yes that's right old kids. Certainly that is a contradiction or a misnomer. The word "kids" implies youth, young children and old, well old speaks for itself. I am often reminded of the song from Fiddler On The Roof, "Sunrise, Sunset." Listen carefully to the words and you will know exactly what I mean.

My kids have hair that is thinning and even showing a hint of gray. Two of the boys are going bald and one has a receding hairline. My lovely daughter is looking forward to menopause when she can stop with all the cramps. She has already begun to dye her hair. I can't quite imagine how this happened especially to one so young but it's true. It's almost as though they grew up when I wasn't looking. Sometimes things like that come to pass, you know just when you don't expect something, wham, something happens and you are completely surprised.

Well, that's what happened here. I turned around and there they were, all grown up. I am sure other folks must feel the same but when it happens and you realize when it happens it is a very personal, intimidating thing.

As far as I am concerned I am still the young mom looking after her brood of children and pleased as punch at how much fun it is to be the mom. It was our decision that I would remain home while the children were growing and that's precisely what I did. I did all the things some women would find irritating but for me I loved it.

I was the homemaker and it was fun. I shoveled snow with my snow "angels," I planted flowers with little hands pulling them out as fast as I was putting them in. I woke in the middle of the night with a sick child and knew I did not have to scurry around for an emergency sitter or take a personal or vacation day from work, I baked tons and tons of cookies, I even tried my hand at making jelly and canning vegetables. I played in backyard tents and spent days and days washing after our family camping escapades.

Now that doesn't mean every moment of every day was glorious or that I didn't sometimes feel like I should be out there in the professional world. There were lots of days and moments when I questioned my decision and would have given anything to be sitting in an office or back in the schoolroom or even back in college. However, upon reflection I realize that this time, those precious years were all mine. They went so quickly and now only live in my memories and of course, in the fading old time movies and slides we took. Every once in while we'll get out the old movie projector and look at them. We laugh and talk about who remembers what and mourn the loss of the ones whose faces now only belong in the old movies.

Having old kids is different to be sure. At times, they give me advice and tell me what to do. And sometimes, just sometimes I take their advice. I also try very hard to let them be themselves. They have a right to follow their dreams and become who they are and not just my children. It's not always easy to do. I realize that they too will make mistakes and hopefully learn from them.

I realize they too will look back on their lives one day and have a few regrets. I realize they too will know some of the greatest joys and also some of the deepest sorrows.

So many very wise people have written all through the ages about children and parents and the unique relationship they have. I have read some of these books, I have pondered their words, I now write some of my own.

When we become parents we kind of plan how we would like our children to turn out, what we would like them to become. What parent does not dream of the attorney, the doctor, the scientist? Isn't it true that our children are the brightest and most promising of any born so far? But I have learned that raising children to become just plain good adults, adults who care for others, who value the family principles they were taught, who strive to leave the planet better than they found it. Ah yes, this is the stuff of a parent's dream and I am privileged to see my children become just that kind of an adult.

I am proud. I genuinely like my old kids and not just love them. I still delight in comments from others who compliment me on my child rearing. I see now in our daughter the same traits in her parenting of her children. She too strives to raise her children based on what we instilled in her. I believe the other children, our sons, if they have children will do the same.

I watch and listen. I smile. I think I did a good job.

The Song Bird

The Song Bird

On the morning of dad's death a little bird appeared right outside of my door. The day was still early and sunlight was not to arrive for many hours. I had come from darkness, the place where dad had died and my heart was shrouded in the color of death. It was strange driving alone, my mind racing with emotions, continuing thoughts of what had just happened, my heart heavy with sadness and the finality of it all.

It was a time that I felt so alone. Mom had been escorted from the death room by my oldest son and his wife. They along with my husband had come to be with us in those first few moments after dad had passed away. He was still there, I could see him and yet he was gone. Gently the nurse came to mom and I and told us, "Your dad has passed." When we went to his side his arms were outstretched as though hoping for one last embrace, his body still warm and comforting to us.

Mom and I had spent the last week with dad in his room. When other family members had gone for the night we would remain with him, holding his hand and quietly talking to him. Mom would rub his head every so gently just as dad always liked. This last night with us everyone came to see him. There was his son and family and the grandchildren and great grandchildren. After everyone had gone mom and I crawled into bed together, tired and weary. We told each other that we would rest just for a few moments before returning to dad's bedside.

Now it was over and I was alone in the car, alone with my thoughts, the tears held as though it was not yet time to shed them. They would come later.

As I left the car and walked toward the door I could hear the lilting sound of a song bird. I turned to see if I could catch a glimpse of the bird and much to my surprise there he was chirping and singing as if to let me know he was there. Strange I thought to myself, strange to hear and see this bird at this hour and in the darkness.

Throughout the morning as the family gathered one after another would stop, listen and mention the bird's presence. Knowing how much dad had loved birds, we were convinced that dad was somehow with us at this time and in this place.

In the two months after dad died the bird remained our constant companion. He sat right outside our breakfast window or on the handle of the rusty old wheelbarrow in the yard. He seemed to venture only so far as our nearest neighbor's house. His song could be heard throughout the day.

As time passed the song was less frequent. Now there were times when the bird was nowhere to be found. Once in a while we would look to see if we could see him and we would stop, listening for the song. The bird and the song were gone. Try as I may, I could not stop the tears. Months after dad left us I finally cried. Why did it take so long? Why would the absence of a tiny bird bring forth the sobs of a lonely daughter?

During the past months I wondered why the bird had remained close by. I did not see that it carried anything in it's mouth nor did it fly to a sheltered nest located in a nearby tree. I am convinced that the bird remained with us for only one purpose, the song he sang. I have always referred to the bird as a male, always a he. It has never crossed my mind that it might have been something else. This bird came to be here, some might say it was sent, some might call it dad's spirit, some might negate the whole thing, "it's only a bird singing, nothing more."

A mantle of snow still blankets the ground ensuring that spring will not arrive for some weeks. There are few birds to be seen but already I am shopping for a few bird feeders for the yard. I am determined to encourage birds to come and stay with us, I am hoping to see and to hear the voice of the messenger, "I am fine, I am happy, I am singing."

Business Cards

Business Cards

I have boxes, and boxes and more boxes of business cards that are no longer useful. Why I brought them home when my tenure was finished at the last three places of employment I don't really know? It must be that I certainly internalized mom's advice not to waste anything and to find a place and purpose for everything. I figured that I might use them (the back of them) as identifiers for pictures in photo albums, they would be all of the same height and width and might lend some attractiveness and uniformity to each picture dialog.

It is now almost five years since the first box came home. I was employed in a utility company that was bought out by a huge conglomerate and my position was eliminated. Home I came with a carton full of desk items, the family pictures, names and email addresses for other so called terminated employees, plants and the usual accumulation of belongings found on employee desks and in offices everywhere. Although I was sad, I did have another job to go to and was looking forward to a better position, higher salary and a secure future.

The following week I carted the box to my new job in a start up company. I knew this would be the job that would ensure a certain retirement, I just knew it. But alas again, a year later we were called into a conference room and greeted with, "We are sorry to inform you . . ." Here we go again. Pack up the box, grab the business cards and make the call to your husband, "I was terminated today. I am on my way home. Yes, I think you better come and drive me, I'm crying."

After this job I had plenty of time to take out boxes of photos and begin to place them in new albums and of course, label each picture by writing on the back of a business card. This proved to be a relaxing endeavor and mom was delighted to see that I was indeed using the old business cards for this purpose. I was bound and determined to organize my life one way or another. By the time I secured a new job my supply of business cards was dwindling. They were not all gone but a dent had been made, I was making progress personally and professionally.

In between jobs as I went from interview to interview I would accumulate a stack of business cards as almost each interviewer handed me their card on the way out. "Here's my business card, you should hear from me within a week. Thank you for coming." Ok, Ok now I have your card, you must be interested in me or so I thought. Sometimes I would have to ask for a card, on those occasions I was convinced that maybe they were not really interested but it was my intention to at least keep the card for reference.

My home desk was beginning to look like a lady on the move, new business cards were placed in my rolodex—this was surely a sign of progress.

When I finally secured a new job again, my third in as many years, I was approached by the secretary asking how I would like my name spelled on my business card. Ah, thank God, at last I'm somebody again, I have a business card. Now I could again join the ranks of those who utter the words, "Here's my business card, give me a call." I brought some home, I placed some in a small plastic case in my purse, I put some in a brief case and the rest I proudly displayed on my office desk. I could hardly wait to hear the words, "Do you have a business card?"

After a year on the job, you guessed it, I was again greeted with the words, "I am sorry to say . . ." Can this be happening again, can I be packing up my desk, putting my pictures and business cards into a box to cart home, can I be once again the owner of useless, outdated, good for nothing business cards?" This time it took longer for me to take them out of the box. It was harder to look at the words on the card that told the world who I was. How would people know who I am now? Who would ask, "Do you have a business card?"

Rummaging through piles of old papers and stacks of files in the basement I come across more business cards. Some belong to my husband, some friends and some from old, now forgotten business contacts. These I discard with ease. These are not mine, they do not represent who I am, or who I was or even who I would like to be. I don't even use them for the purpose of identifying photos.

Someone told me to just make up a business card. Call myself a consultant, give myself a title, make up a company name and logo and then go out and "peddle" myself. I don't want to. I am determined to secure a new position, one requiring the printing of a business card, one where I will hear the words, "How would you like your name spelled on your business card?"

In the meantime here I am, opening yet another box of photos, writing the identifying words on the back of the business card, wondering how long it will take to use up my supply, how long it will take until the world knows once again who I am?

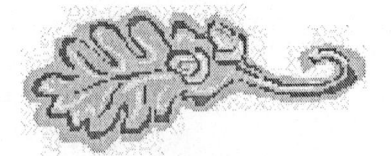

The First One

The First One

Christmas is coming and this will be our first year without Dad. How strange I think as I start to wrap presents and bake cookies. How strange when I think he will not be here to open his gifts and to delight in the squeals of his beloved great grandchildren. How strange not to have him appear at our door in his Christmas garb; plaid trousers, red sport jacket, Christmas socks and tie. One year he even wore a bow tie made out of felt in the shape of holly leaves, red berries and all.

You knew Christmas was coming because mom and dad would begin their annual trek around the state to view the myriad of Christmas decorations in stores, garden centers, and on town greens. This also would be the time of parties and open houses for the varied organizations they belonged to. They would inevitably come home with more Christmas "stuff" to add to their already bulging collection of ornaments for tree, mantle, door and floor.

I could not help but wonder why they insisted on buying more "stuff" when they had a house full of "stuff." I kept thinking that at their age they did not need to add to any collections or decorations. They already had so much. But following their pattern to collect things one year they decided that a collection of Santa's would be nice.

Off they went to a shop and bought many of the Santa's that represent different years. Mom said they would buy only one and keep adding to the collection each year. The story goes that dad looked at her and said, "For God's sake Mike you are ninety, don't you think you should buy as many as you would like," referring I am sure to her age and physical condition. She replied that she would buy some now and some later, ah, the power of positive thinking!

Home came the Santas to take their place alongside the precious ornaments collected or handed down through the years. Looking back at this activity I can see just how into life they were and how determined to live each and every day with an outlook only found in the youngest and healthiest of family and friends.

Their decorations consisted of fragile glass ornaments from their first Christmas trees that resembled those found in antique shops at this time of the year. There also was dad's old train and assorted toys from his childhood.

How proud and thrilled they were to take out the boxes and boxes and more boxes of Christmas delights. Of course, everything had a story to tell and as the ornaments were stripped of their wrappings the stories would begin. "This was on dad's first tree. It was made by his Aunt Aurore when he was nine years old." It was a hand colored Santa with movable arms and legs. Immediately you did the math. If dad was born in 1911 and he was nine when the ornament was made, the ornament would be over eighty years old.

Next came the old metal train and then the wooden circus train, the child's play washing tub, ironing board and clothes. Mom would contribute her doll's Morris chair and plenty of dolls and doll clothes. "The envy of collectors and antique enthusiasts," we would hear year after year. "Remember, this is to be kept in the family and passed down to each generation and don't forget the story to go with it."

As the years went by and mom and dad became more fragile and incapable of descending into the basement us kids and grandkids would go down for them and gather the precious cargo and bring it up to them. "Watch out and don't put anything heavy on the boxes. Bring up all of them. Did you see the carton with the crèche and angels?" And so it went until all of the boxes were finally in the living room.

For me it was easy to remember all the treasures, I saw them year after year. For my children it was a different story. They were enthralled with the stories and the unwrapping of such treasures. "Mom, these don't look like our ornaments, do they? Hey, look at this one. Grammy B can I have this one when you get old and don't have a tree any more?"

In the last few years the job became more tiring. Just the thought of unwrapping things was almost too much, but carry on they did. Even until the end. Last year dad spent Christmas in the hospital and was unable to come home. True to the custom of their home, mom asked our oldest son to go into the basement to bring up some boxes. She arranged the tree, the ceramic crèche and angels and placed the wreath on the door. "I want it to be ready when grandpa comes home. He loves Christmas and would be disappointed if the house was not decorated."

Then she went to the hospital. "We'll have Christmas when you come home," she told him. Dad just stared at her. I think he knew he would not be home for the holidays. There would be no parties, no bow ties or stories. Mom kept the decorations up for quite some time and one day called us to the house. "Help me take down the things. I want you to take them home with you. We will not need them again."

The Christmas Tree

The Christmas Tree

"It's a little small but it'll do." With those words mom gave the Ok for the tree to be placed on dad's grave. She was referring to the tree that I had purchased at the annual Church Christmas Fair the day before, it was there in the corner with a $1.00 tag on it and somehow I just thought it would be appropriate for dad. I scoured the table for ornaments that we could place on it, ones that could withstand the New England winter weather including snow and wind. I chose plastic icicles, a few tiny figures in wood and a sparkling plastic angel for the top who hung there precariously.

This tree was so different from those that had been a part of dad's Christmases for years and years. It was not the feather tree his mom purchased for his first Christmas from Howland Hughes, an old time department store in his hometown. Nor was it the ceiling high fresh trees of my childhood, the ones dad would hide in the garage so us kids would not see them and he and mom could drag it into the house after we fell asleep on Christmas Eve.

It was not the familiar tree that we enjoyed in later years. This tree was always decked out in ornaments from his and mom's childhood, a truly magical tree envied by those who had the chance to enjoy it during a visit to his home. Under the tree were placed the antique toys, old tin trains, dolls in Morris chairs, tiny circus animals and selected and prized wooden toys.

I was not sure how mom would feel about this tree and the whole idea of bringing it to dad. But it was something I needed to do. Something I wanted to do. I didn't just want to get one of the typical grave decorations, the greens and a few plastic flowers. I wanted a tree that we decorated and we placed there.

The "first time" ceremony would take place after church on

Sunday. My daughter and grand daughters would be there to take part in this new Christmas tradition. Luckily no snow had fallen and we were able to move easily across the damp uneven grass to the barren brown gravesite. The tiny tree was lovingly placed there by dad's precious great grand daughters and their mom. It was clear that this tree would need a little help just to stand up so both girls set out to hunt for rocks large enough place around it.

The littlest one scratched in the dirt to make a spot to hold the tree stand and as they worked diligently to ensure the tree would stand upright, I was carried back to past Christmases. My eyes were misting as I watched these two small figures and remembered my time with my daddy.

"Grammy, how does it look? Do you think it will stand up?" "Why of course it will," I replied. I did not want this to be a sad time, no, I wanted it to be like Christmases past when tree decorating and family traditions were the highlight of the day. I wanted it to be like the rest of them.

But I knew just as the little ones and mom and my daughter did, this was not like the rest of them. This ceremony would color our feelings and would remind us of the emptiness we felt. Mom held up valiantly and did not shed a tear. My daughter spoke a few words and the children continued to "decorate" the grave. Next on the list was a wooden Santa surrounded with colorful wooden packages in bright colors. Again the littlest one bent to place it on the grave.

Just when I thought my feelings would come pouring out and my tears could no longer be hidden, I heard the voices of the children.

"There you go grandpa," said one. Adding to this was, "Here's your own tree. Now you will be ok Papa." My heart skipped and my breath held as I listened in the stillness of the graveyard. It was time to leave, time to help mom into the car, time to return home. How was mom? Was this too much for her?

"We are putting up the Christmas tree at your grandma's house. Would you like to come and help us?" Mom called to the children and again voiced the invitation. "Can we go mom, can we go to grandma's and put up the tree?" "Yes, that would be fine" replied my daughter.

As we headed for the car I turned once more to see the little tree and the wooden Santa Claus. "We're going home now dad, you have your tree and as Sarah Anne would say, 'You'll be alright Papa'."

A Wee One

A Wee One

Just two weeks ago a wee one arrived in my life, a tiny, beautiful package of ultimate joy! This wee one's name is Alexander and although he is technically to live with his parents, our son and daughter-in-law, he lives deep within my heart and soul. I cry as I am greeted with the news of his birth, "We have a son!"

I run to embrace our son and our tears mingle as we hold each other tightly just the two of us alone in our thoughts. I celebrate this wonder of wonders, this miracle, the birth of a first born child, a son. I am drawn back to a time and place different from here yet so alike in the message, "we have a son." My heart remembers his birth, my tears fall as they did then and although my arms hold a man, yet they hold my child, my firstborn, my son.

I realize he must go to the others waiting anxiously in the family area. I know this moment can only be that, a moment. I let him go and watch as he approaches the others and listen again to his words, "We have a son!" Quickly he is surrounded by brothers, sisters, father, and in-laws whose lives have now been forever changed by this birth. I listen to one after another repeat the words, "congratulations," and their tears begin. I watch as he moves from one to the other and accepts the embraces, the tears.

"Oh my child," my heart cries. "Oh my child, you too now know of this miracle, this beautiful moment, this life changing event." You who are bone of bone and blood of my blood. Now this new child is yours, savor it, remember it, store it in your heart so you can always know this moment in time.

Throughout the next few days we visit the miracle place often. We silently steal into the room and watch with joy the new parents and their child. We watch as they cuddle him, nurse him, change diapers. We watch how they look at him and at each other, we are enthralled.

We listen to the sounds of this wee one and the sounds of his parents. I try to remind myself that this is their time, the words they speak to him and to each other are not my words, nor should they be. They have created and brought this child into their world and although I am the grandmother, they are the parents.

They are the ones to teach this child, they are the ones whose words and actions can help to determine the providence of this child's life, they are the wise ones with their child. We often read about the role of grandparent, the special bond and connection between a child and a grandparent. I intend to forge that bond just as I have with my other precious grandchildren, I intend to be there for Alexander too. But my role and my life are not theirs, nor should I become more important than parents. This is their time.

I am just delighted just to be grandma, to be able to view this tiny family, this beginning, this birth of their first child, a son. I am delighted to be included in the triangle of parent, child, grandparent. I am delighted to call this wee one mine.

Showing Off

Showing Off

I love showing off. I just love it when someone stops me and says, "Oh, how beautiful." I am thoroughly delighted when I can parade around town, or in a store, or doctor's office and feel people staring at me. I am not the least bit bashful or shy. I just feel like strutting around watching for someone to approach or for someone to recognize me. And of course, I get just what I am looking for.

Inevitably someone turns, looks straight at me and smiles. "Good," I think, "they have the right idea." I almost giggle like a young schoolgirl with her first grown up outfit or her first pair of high heels. Remember those days? You could hardly wait to put them on and march out into the world looking and hoping that people would cast their eyes your way.

That's it, I'm not just walking, but rather strolling or sauntering, taking just the right amount of time with each step to ensure everyone gets a good look. If no one is around I quickly move myself to where people are, gradually placing myself in their direct view. There I think, "now look at me."

And true to my prediction the stares begin; the smile first, then the walking toward me to get a better look and then the compliments start. What more can I ask for? I am on display. And of course, as is customarily the way, others turn to stare also and begin to move closer. Now I've got you.

Because it is still winter there are clothes to undo and hats to remove. Quickly I remove the outer garment and hat so as to provide a clear view. I am reveling in this activity. "Oh how beautiful," replies one lady. "You must be so happy." Someone else comes close and says, "It looks like you are enjoying this." Someone else chimes in, "you are very lucky."

Alex, my new infant grandson comfortably cradled in my arms, and I respond. He, eyes closed and looking so angelic first gives forth a tiny grimace then a smile and I beam with delight. Then the questions begin. "How old is he? Is this your first? How many grandchildren do you have?" Alex and I play right into our roles, me as the adoring grandmother, he as the precious new child. "He is just a month old," I answer. "No, he is not the first but oh so very precious, a true miracle for us." And so it goes. People stare, we respond. People share the moment, the miracle.

Nothing can compare to this, not my first pair of high heels, not my wedding day, not anything. This is a day to strut and stroll, a day to ask for and receive compliments, a day to share the joy.

Other grandparents smile in such a way as to say, "I know just how you feel."

A showoff I am and proud of it! What better way to get people to stare, to smile and to offer congratulations? What better way to show off? Move over all you young ladies with new high heels and grown up outfits. Little Alex and I are here and there is no competing with us!

Post Script Or Four Is Never Enough

Post Script or Four is Never Enough

We have four children, children who came early in our marriage and quite close together in their arrivals. We hadn't really had a conversation about having children or the plan for the arrival of each one. There was no discussion, no thought until it happened. Now wouldn't you think that after the first one's arrival only nine months and two weeks after our marriage and the second one on our second anniversary that we would "look into the matter" and take steps to alter the next arrivals?

Not really. We just went about our business and let nature take it's course. Some would question our thinking processes and wonder why anyone would do what we did. But in the end it proved to be a fun time, albeit a hectic life style. I did stay home from work for the first years and that helped to alleviate some of the stress of this growing family life.

When our children were a little more on their way to being grown up we had a new arrival. She came not by the normal course of action, she didn't even come by adoption. She just arrived and has been a part of our family ever since. We have been able to watch her grow from a teenager into a young woman, a wife and a mother. Along the way her life and ours and those of our children and grandchildren have become intertwined as only a family can become. Each member an integral part of the whole. This young lady named Melanie became for all practical purposes our daughter. As the years went by her role was like those of her siblings and a constant reminder of our responsibility to each other in the family dynamics of everyday life.

We got to share in her growing, her struggles, her joyful moments. We helped her as parents help children with material goods, guidance and a great deal of love. I believe there were even times when a good talking to was in order. Melanie is today a joy, a young lady with a family of her own.

And through Melanie and her husband we have become grandparents again. Both Meghan and Brian come into our lives as did our other grandchildren with joyful anticipation and brought newness, and a sense of family continuity.

Our oldest son John William, our daughter Heather Ann and our other two sons, Steven Matthew and Christopher Adam never lost their place in our family. They, like my husband and I just welcomed her and that was that. Each of our biological children have brought such joy and delight that adding one more child just seemed the right thing to do.

Today most families are planned, most children arrive when their parents are ready. But for me and for my husband I think of each of our arrivals as a sort of Christmas morning; a time for real surprise and amazing unbridled joy!

There are never enough children for us to love. And so it is with my writing. There are never enough stories. So many thoughts, so many memories, so many more stories to write and to leave for others to find and read. So much to be said, so many promises to keep.

BVG